THE
COLTONS
COMANCHE BLOOD

Welcome to Black Arrow, Oklahoma—
the birthplace of a proud, passionate clan who
would risk everything for love, family and honor.

Jared Colton:
He never hung around one place for too long, but
the new town hero had gained the attention of the
only woman who could tempt him to stay…at least
a little while longer.

Kerry WindWalker:
She'd steered clear of Jared Colton because of his
bad-boy reputation, but his heroic gesture had her
wondering if the avowed bachelor could become
a true family man.

Gloria WhiteBear:
Would the secret past of the Oklahoma Coltons'
matriarch come back to haunt her grandchildren?

Bram Colton:
A man of honor and Comanche pride, the revered
sheriff of Black Arrow had been kept busy since
strange happenings started occurring in town….

Dear Reader,

There's more than one way to enjoy the summer. By picking up this month's Silhouette Special Edition romances, you will find an emotional escape that is sure to touch your heart and leave you believing in happily-ever-after!

I am pleased to introduce a gripping tale of true love and family from celebrated author Stella Bagwell. In *White Dove's Promise*, which launches a six-book spin-off—plus a Christmas story collection—of the popular COLTONS series, a dashing Native American hero has trouble staying in one place, until he finds himself entangled in a soul-searing embrace with a beautiful single mother, who teaches him about roots…and lifelong passion.

No "keeper" shelf is complete without a gem from Joan Elliott Pickart. In *The Royal MacAllister*, a woman seeks her true identity and falls madly in love with a *true* royal! In *The Best Man's Plan*, bestselling and award-winning author Gina Wilkins delights us with a darling love story between a lovely shop owner and a wealthy businessman, who set up a fake romance to trick the tabloids…and wind up falling in love for real!

Lisa Jackson's *The McCaffertys: Slade* features a lady lawyer who comes home and faces a heartbreaker hero, who desperately wants a chance to prove his love to her. In *Mad Enough To Marry*, Christie Ridgway entertains us with an adorable tale of that *maddening* love that happens only when two kindred spirits must share the same space. Be sure to pick up Arlene James's *His Private Nurse*, where a single father falls for the feisty nurse hired to watch over him after a suspicious accident. You won't want to miss it!

Each month, Silhouette Special Edition delivers compelling stories of life, love and family. I wish you a relaxing summer and happy reading.

Sincerely,

Karen Taylor Richman
Senior Editor

Please address questions and book requests to:
Silhouette Reader Service
U.S.: 3010 Walden Ave., P.O. Box 1325, Buffalo, NY 14269
Canadian: P.O. Box 609, Fort Erie, Ont. L2A 5X3

Stella Bagwell

WHITE DOVE'S PROMISE

Silhouette®

SPECIAL EDITION™

Published by Silhouette Books

America's Publisher of Contemporary Romance

Special thanks and acknowledgment are given to Stella Bagwell for her contribution to THE COLTONS series.

To the two men in my life.
My husband, Harrell, and our son, Jason.

 SILHOUETTE BOOKS

ISBN 0-373-24478-9

WHITE DOVE'S PROMISE

STELLA BAGWELL

Recently Stella and her husband of thirty years moved from the hills of Oklahoma to Seadrift, Texas, a sleepy little fishing town located on the coastal bend. Stella says the water, the tropical climate and the seabirds make it a lovely place to let her imagination soar and to put the stories in her head down on paper.

She and her husband have one son, Jason, who lives and teaches high school math in nearby Port Lavaca.

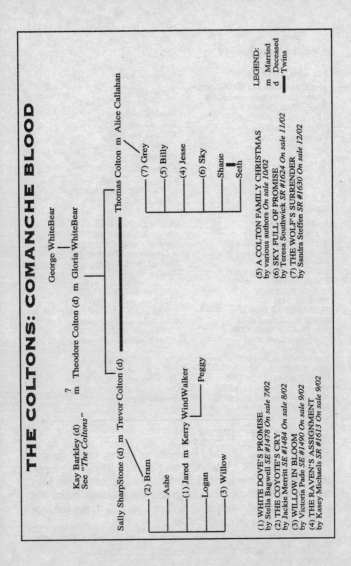

THE COLTONS: COMANCHE BLOOD

George WhiteBear

Kay Barkley (d)
See "The Coltons"

? m Theodore Colton (d) m Gloria WhiteBear

Sally SharpStone (d) m Trevor Colton (d)

Thomas Colton m Alice Callahan

(2) Bram

Ashe

(1) Jared m Kerry WindWalker

Logan   Peggy

(3) Willow

(7) Grey

(5) Billy

(4) Jesse

(6) Sky

Shane

Seth

(1) WHITE DOVE'S PROMISE
by Stella Bagwell SE #1478 On sale 7/02

(2) THE COYOTE'S CRY
by Jackie Merritt SE #1484 On sale 8/02

(3) WILLOW IN BLOOM
by Victoria Pade SE #1490 On sale 9/02

(4) THE RAVEN'S ASSIGNMENT
by Kasey Michaels SR #1613 On sale 9/02

(5) A COLTON FAMILY CHRISTMAS
by various authors On sale 10/02

(6) SKY FULL OF PROMISE
by Teresa Southwick SR #1624 On sale 11/02

(7) THE WOLF'S SURRENDER
by Sandra Steffen SR #1630 On sale 12/02

LEGEND:
m Married
d Deceased
▬ Twins

Chapter One

"Lunch at your desk. At this rate, you're going to have burnout before you reach the age of thirty."

Unaware that anyone else had entered her small office, Kerry WindWalker jerked her head up from the promissory note she'd been typing to see one of Liberty National Bank's loan officers standing at the corner of her desk.

Smiling at the tall, gray-haired man, she said, "I'm behind, Clarence. It's Monday. Everyone seems to be broke on Mondays."

With a rueful grin, he placed more work on the corner of her already loaded desk. "Reality hits when the weekend is over. But it doesn't mean you need to work through your lunch hour. Have you eaten anything with that?" he asked, inclining his head toward the half-empty soda bottle sitting near her typewriter.

Kerry shook her head. "Not yet. But I will. I have a sandwich waiting for me back in the break room."

Clarence glanced at his wristwatch. "It's almost two," he gently scolded. "Turn that machine off and go eat. Now."

Three years ago, Kerry had returned to Black Arrow, Oklahoma, and, shortly after, landed a position there in the loan department at Liberty National. Back then Clarence had been the first to welcome her into the fold and make her feel at ease. It was her first important job after acquiring her business degree and his kind support had meant a lot to a young girl fresh out of college and desperately needing a paycheck. Since then the older man had become someone she could truly call a friend. For that reason she always took extra time to see that his loans were processed before anyone else's. "But Mr.—"

He waved a dismissive hand at her protests. "Mr. Whoever can wait. Including me."

With a shrug of surrender, she switched off the power on the typewriter, then rose from her chair. "Okay, I'm on my way," she told him as she absently brushed at the wrinkles in her slim, beige skirt.

The loan officer paused at the door to make sure she was following him out of the small office. Kerry was about to ask him if he'd stopped to have his own lunch when the phone on her desk rang.

"Forget it," Clarence prompted. "It's probably Landers wanting to know if you've finished the papers on the Crawford loan. He can wait, too."

The fact that Clarence considered her break more important than the wishes of the bank's vice president put a smile on Kerry's face. Since she'd started the job she'd oftentimes worked through breaks and beyond office hours to make sure her work was completed punctually. It was nice to know someone appreciated her dedication, especially someone like Clarence who'd been with the bank for more than twenty years and pulled a considerable amount of weight with the president.

"I'd better get it anyway," she told him. "After all, it's past my lunch break. I'm supposed to be at my desk at this time of the day."

Tucking her short black bob behind her ears, she hurried back to the L-shaped desk and plucked up the ringing phone.

"Kerry WindWalker speaking."

"Kerry! Thank God you finally answered! I thought you might be out and I don't know what to do!"

For a second, the frantic sound of Enola Wind-Walker's voice didn't quite register with Kerry. Her mother never called the bank and interrupted her work.

Kerry's smooth brow was suddenly furrowed as she anxiously gripped the receiver. "Mom? Is that you? Is something wrong?"

"Oh—Kerry—I don't know how to tell you this but—I can't find Peggy."

Kerry's blood suddenly turned to ice water. Peggy was her three-year-old daughter, the very existence of her being.

Trying not to go into instant panic, she said, "Mom, take a deep breath and calm down. Surely, she's around there somewhere. Have you looked under the beds? In all the closets? You know how your granddaughter likes to play hide-and-seek."

Kerry could hear Enola struggling to stifle a sob and the sound shot shards of fear straight through her. At fifty-six, Enola was a strong, steadfast woman. In fact,

Kerry couldn't ever remember seeing her mother rattled, even years ago, when she'd been dealing with an alcoholic husband. For her to be so close to breaking now was enough to tell Kerry that something was terribly wrong.

"I've searched the house," Enola told her. "I've searched the yard. I walked down the road as far as I thought her little legs might be able to go and called to her. If she's hiding, she won't answer. It's been nearly an hour now since I missed her!"

Fear wadding in her throat, Kerry glanced up to see Clarence was still waiting in the doorway. From the anxious expression on his face, the older man had already sensed that something was wrong. "Peggy—my daughter—is missing," she explained to him.

Grim-faced, the loan officer strode quickly over to Kerry's desk. "Have the sheriff's office or city police been notified?" he asked briskly.

Kerry directed her attention back to her mother on the other end of the telephone line. "Mom, have you called any sort of law officials?"

"Yes, I've called Bram Colton—he's not here yet. But most of the neighbors are already out hunting for her. I think—"

Enola continued talking, but Kerry ignored the rest of her words as she shook her head at Clarence and managed to choke out, "She's called the sheriff, but he hasn't arrived at my mother's house yet. Peggy's been missing for nearly an hour."

"Get over there. I'll explain things here for you," he said definitively.

As she watched Clarence hurrying out of the room, she said to her mother as calmly as possible, "I'm leaving the bank now, Mom. Just hang on and I'll be there in a few minutes.''

Outside in the parking lot, Kerry jumped in her car and headed home, to the west outskirts of Black Arrow. Shaded by two huge cottonwoods, the house was old, built in shotgun fashion with a wide porch running the entire width of the front. Throughout the years, the lapped wooden siding had been painted first one color and then another. Presently, it was a bleached-out yellow with equally faded brown trim. The shingles needed replacing, the front screen door was warped and one end of the porch floor sagged. But to Kerry the old place had always been home and so far it was the only home that little Peggy had known.

Even though the WindWalker property wasn't far from the city limits, the road running in front of the house had never been paved. Gravel spewed from Kerry's tires as she brought her compact car to a stop in the short driveway.

Watching from the porch, a petite woman dressed in jeans and a blue T-shirt with a single black braid lying against her back raced out to meet her daughter. Tears had dried on her cheeks, but were threatening to spill from her eyes once again as she grabbed onto Kerry's shoulders and hugged her fiercely.

''Oh Mom, what happened? Where do you think she is?''

Releasing her hold on Kerry, Enola wiped her eyes and began in a broken, trembling voice, ''I'm so sorry, honey, it's all my fault. Peggy and I were outside—in the back at the vegetable garden. I heard the phone ringing and ran into the kitchen to get it. I told her to wait for me there—that I'd be right back. She seemed to be happy and preoccupied with pulling radishes and

I was only gone a minute. Two at the most. But as soon as I stepped into the backyard again, she was nowhere to be seen.''

Kerry momentarily closed her brown eyes and sent up yet another silent prayer for her daughter to be found safe and sound. "Don't blame yourself, Mom. We both know how adventurous Peggy is and you can't keep your eyes on her every second of the day.''

"Yes, but I should have made her come with me—''

Determined to hold herself and her mother together, Kerry took Enola firmly by the arm and led her toward the house. "Right now it won't do anyone any good for you to be worrying about ifs or should haves, Mom. Let's just try to figure out where she might have gone. Was Fred with her?''

The spotted bird dog was only twelve weeks old, but already he acted as if he were grown and would run off and hunt whenever the urge struck him. Peggy was infatuated with the little guy and Kerry had the sinking feeling her daughter had followed the pup away from the house.

"He was there with us when I went to answer the phone. Do you think she's wandered off with him?''

Kerry nodded, then drew in a shaky breath as another, more frightening thought entered her mind. "Unless, God forbid—you didn't see a car or anyone walking past here when you went to answer the phone?''

Enola shook her head emphatically. "No. There was no one. I would have heard a car and if anyone had walked near the house, Fred would have been barking up a storm.''

That much was true, Kerry thought with relief, then turned toward the sound of an approaching vehicle just in time to see a white pickup truck with the sheriff's logo emblazoned on the side door wheeling into the driveway then halting beside her car. Immediately she recognized Bram Colton behind the wheel. The young Comanche County sheriff had already built a reputation for getting the job done. Kerry only hoped it held true in this case.

"There's the sheriff," she said to her mother. "Let's go tell him everything you just told me."

A quarter of a mile away from the WindWalker residence, Jared Colton studied the blueprints he'd rolled out on the hood of his truck. He'd been a petroleum engineer for close to ten years now and he'd encountered a few strange jobs now and then, but he'd never seen such a damn mess as this one.

Down through the years most townships had written laws into their civil codes forbidding oil or gas drilling to take place inside city limits. But in the case of Black Arrow, the ordinance hadn't come into being until after the town had grown around several already producing gas wells. A few weeks ago, a gas company had come in to lay new pipe to an old well, but shortly into the job something had gone wrong and the crew had somehow managed to cave in part of the city's drainage system along with blocking the flow of natural gas. Jared's job was to figure out how to get everything open and running as it should be without causing any more loss to city property.

So far he and his crew had slowly uncovered part of the damaged drainage pipes which would eventually be rerouted to miss the gas line. As for the natural gas well itself, it would have to be capped off, then re-drilled from a different direction.

Jared rubbed a thoughtful forefinger against one jaw as he lifted his head and surveyed the mess in front of him. Normally at this time of the day, the place would have been buzzing with workers and machinery, but yesterday's rain showers had made the ground too muddy to work. And even though it was a sunny afternoon today, he still wasn't all that certain the ground would be dry enough to work with any sort of heavy equipment tomorrow. Plus the fact that early May in Oklahoma was apt to produce thunderstorms at the drop of a hat. He'd be lucky if it wasn't raining again tomorrow.

Sighing, he lifted the hard hat from his head and ran a hand through his thick black hair. Being down a day or two wouldn't prevent him from finishing the job in the amount of time allotted in his contract and he'd already put in a hell of a week. Some rest would be good for him and the crew. He might even call Bram and Logan to see if his brothers wanted to have dinner with him tonight.

A fond smile teased the corners of his mouth. The two of them would probably think he was ill. It wasn't often he chose to spend the evening with his brothers rather than a female companion. Both Bram and Logan would find it hard to believe their skirt-chasing brother couldn't think of even one woman in the whole town of Black Arrow that he wanted to spend more than five minutes with.

Jared's thoughts about juicy steaks and brotherly companionship were suddenly interrupted when he felt something tugging on the hem of his jean leg.

Glancing down, he saw a red speckled pup chewing with delight on his leather workboot. "Well, where did you come from, little guy?"

The sound of Jared's voice distracted the pup from his chewing. The dog looked up at him, then backed away and let out a croaky bark. Jared squatted on his heels and with an outstretched hand invited the pup to come closer. "Come here, fella. Let's see if you have a name tag on your collar."

Wary, but overcome with curiosity, the pup sidled closer, then wiggled with delight the moment Jared ran a friendly hand over his sleek head. Fastened to a black leather collar, a metal disc dangled at the front of the dog's throat. Jared angled the silver gray disc so that he could read the letters. Fred was written on one side. A local phone number was on the other.

Rising to his full height, which was just shy of six feet, Jared's gray eyes scanned the open fields around him. The nearest house was at least a quarter mile away. A long distance for a little guy like Fred to travel, he pondered. No doubt someone would be missing the dog soon and be out searching for him.

Jared's cell phone was lying on the truck seat. The least he could do was call the number on the pup's collar and inform the owner that the dog was safe.

He opened the truck door to retrieve the telephone, then realized he'd have to look at Fred's collar again to get the number. Slipping the fliptop phone in his shirt pocket, he turned back to grab the dog, only to find the animal scampering off toward the maze of open trenches.

"Fred! Come back here," he called.

The dog ignored him, so Jared tried whistling. The sound produced a bark, but the dog still refused to return.

Muttering a curse under his breath and wondering why he was taking the time to bother with the animal,

Jared started after him. As soon as Fred spotted his approach, he began to bark with loud enthusiasm into the open trench as though he'd just treed a coon in a hollow log. Only this time the log was a smashed drainpipe.

"Okay, fella, I know you think you're out on a hunt, but you've got to go home, wherever that is," he said to the dog.

Ignoring him, Fred continued to bark and whine, forcing Jared to jump into the ditch to go after him. It was then he saw the little footprints in the damp earth. Tiny human imprints leading up to the drainage pipe.

If there had been a set of adult tracks alongside, Jared wouldn't have thought too much about the fact that someone had been out here looking over the excavation site. Working this close to town, he was surprised there hadn't been more people snooping around the diggings than the two teenage boys he'd chased away last week.

Uneasy at this sudden discovery of another type of visitor, he bent down and peered into the pipe. Nothing but a little mud and water settled at the bottom. He glanced behind him, hoping that the tracks would tell him that the little feet had turned back around and headed away from the work site. They didn't.

Grim-faced, he jumped out of the ditch and followed the pipe until it ended and the ditch opened up again. The footprints reappeared in the mud, along with the pup's.

Quickly, Jared followed the tracks until they disappeared into a slim cavity created between a slab of earth and another damaged drainpipe.

Oh no, he thought sickly. Surely the child hadn't squeezed into such a dark, narrow opening. But from the looks of the tracks in the bottom of the ditch that was exactly what he'd done.

Sensing that Jared was finally on the right track and getting the message, Fred barked excitedly into the small opening while clawing at the damp earth. The dog's actions said as much or more to Jared than the footprints. His little buddy had disappeared and he'd been waiting around for someone to help him find him.

Not bothering with the telephone number on Fred's collar, Jared pulled out the cell phone and dialed the sheriff's office.

"I need to speak to the sheriff," he quickly told the female dispatcher, adding, "This is his brother, Jared Colton."

"I'm sorry, Mr. Colton, but the sheriff is out on an emergency right now. Would you like to leave a message?"

Jared silently cursed at the rotten timing. "No. I want you to radio him right this minute and tell him I think I have an emergency on my hands. A child has gone into a drainage system west of town."

"A child? Oh. Okay, give me your location and I'll radio him at once."

Jared told her the location of the work site and also supplied her with the number to his cell phone. In just a matter of moments the telephone rang and his brother was on the end of the line.

"Jared, I just got your message. I have half my force out looking for a three-year-old girl right now. She's been missing for nearly two hours. You think you've found her?"

A three-year-old girl! Somehow Jared had expected Fred's young buddy to be a boy. The idea of a soft, sweet little girl exploring a muddy ditch with an adventurous bird dog had never entered his mind.

"I'm out here at the work site now, Bram, and I've found her dog and where she's been, but not the child. I think you'd better get over here pronto."

"I'll be there in five minutes," he assured him.

"Uh, Bram," he said, before his brother had a chance to hang up, "does the little girl belong to someone we know?"

"Yeah. You probably remember the WindWalkers. It's Kerry's daughter."

Surprise jolted him. The last thing Jared had heard about Kerry WindWalker was that she'd gone to Charlottesville to attend the University of Virginia. No one had told him she'd married or that she'd returned to Black Arrow. But then he'd not asked anyone about the young Comanche girl who'd once snubbed her nose at him. Proud, prim and very beautiful. That's the way he remembered Kerry WindWalker. He wondered if marriage and motherhood had changed her.

The persistent buzz in his ear finally made Jared realize his brother had hung up the phone. Disgusted with himself for letting his thoughts stray, he snapped the instrument shut and slipped it back into his pocket. Now wasn't the time to be thinking about the one woman in Black Arrow who'd resisted his charms. At the moment, he had a smaller female to worry about.

Three minutes later, Bram's pickup truck arrived, followed by several deputies in squad cars. Immediately behind the lawmen, local residents began to pour onto the scene in cars and on foot.

Jared climbed out of the ditch and hurried to meet his brother, but halfway there a petite woman dressed in a slim beige skirt, black blouse and black high heels raced up to him and frantically grabbed his arm.

"Where is she? Where is my baby?"

Jared stared down at Kerry WindWalker's desperate face and wondered how the added years had somehow made her even more beautiful than he remembered. Shiny crow-black hair, high molded cheekbones, honey-brown skin, and eyes the color of sweet chocolate suggested she was half Comanche like himself. While her dusky pink lips reminded him she'd been the one girl he'd always wanted to kiss, but had never been given the chance.

"Kerry—" For a moment her name was all he could manage to say until the fear widening her brown eyes forced him to continue. "I'm not sure where your daughter is. I've followed her tracks and from the looks of things she's entered one of the drainage ditches and hasn't come out."

Jared watched her mouth fall open. At the same time he could feel her small fingers tightening in a death grip around his forearm. She was terrified and rightly so. Yet she was holding herself together with the courage of a Comanche warrior. Admiration flowed through him, along with the desperate urge to help her.

"What do you mean? Hasn't come out of what?" she flung the questions at him.

Before Jared could explain, Bram, dressed in a tan uniform and sheriff's badge, joined them. The oldest of the five Colton siblings, Bram was only an inch taller than Jared and shared the same athletic build and black hair. Yet the similarities stopped there. Where Jared's eyes were gray and usually full of playful mischief, Bram's were black and serious. At the moment, the two brothers were both tight-lipped with anxiety.

"You'd better show me where she went in, Jared," Bram said, then to Kerry he added, "You can come with us. But tell your mother and the rest that they must stay back and out of the way."

Nodding, Kerry left them momentarily and hurried over to briefly explain the situation to her mother. As the two men waited for her, Jared said, "I don't like the looks of this, Bram. The girl has ventured into a spot where we haven't started working yet. It's a safe bet to say that the drainpipes have probably broken and shifted into all sorts of directions and turned the whole thing into a treacherous maze. She's probably crawled inside one of them and can't find her way out."

"Damn it, why wasn't someone out here? Where's your work crew anyway?"

Jared didn't allow Bram's sharp questions to get under his skin. His older brother took the responsibility of his sheriff's position very seriously and he was committed to keeping everyone in Comanche County safe.

"It rained yesterday, remember? I let the crew off," Jared explained. "As for someone guarding the place, that responsibility lies with the gas company and they apparently didn't want to be out the extra expense. The yellow tape is supposed to keep people away from the danger."

Bram's lips twisted with disapproval as he eyed the yellow caution tape that roped the perimeter of the well site. "Yeah," he said with sarcasm. "That's sure going to keep the kids out of this accident waiting to happen."

"Believe me, Bram, I tried to warn the gas company. Right after we started digging up the place I asked them to supply a night watchman at the very least, but they refused. His salary would have been a hell of a lot cheaper than the lawsuit that might come out of this.''

Kerry rejoined them just as Jared finished speaking. Her expression was grave, but hopeful as her gaze encompassed both men.

''Mother will keep the friends and relatives back,'' she assured Bram.

The sheriff nodded at her, then motioned for Jared to lead them to the spot where the child had entered the drainage pipe.

Instinctively, Jared took Kerry by the arm. ''The ground is rough and slippery,'' he gently warned her. ''So watch your step.''

Kerry realized she must appear ridiculous in her skirt and high heels, but she couldn't help it. Ever since she'd raced home from the bank, she'd not had time to draw a deep breath, much less change her clothes. Already her panty hose were lined with runners from searching through a clump of blackberry vines. Coppery-colored stains smeared the front of her shirt and skirt from leaning over the rusty pieces of an old car that had been junked not far from here. But what she looked like to this man or anyone else didn't matter one iota. Getting her daughter back safely in her arms was all she cared about. And she had to believe that was going to happen. She had to. Otherwise, she would simply break apart.

''How long has it been since you found the dog and the tracks, Jared?'' Bram asked.

''Not long. Ten minutes, maybe. Couldn't be much more than that.''

The three of them had reached the point where the footsteps had finally disappeared. Fred was still there in the bottom of the ditch. Apparently the pup had worn himself out and was now stretched out on his belly, his muzzle resting on his paws as he diligently watched the small crevice for a sign of Peggy.

The moment Kerry spotted the dog, her composure cracked. Her hand flew to her mouth to stifle the sob that was burning her throat.

"Oh God—is she—is she down there? In that?"

The agony in her voice tore a hole right through Jared. The need to comfort her crowded everything else from his mind, making him instinctively reach for her shoulders and pull her lightly against his chest. "She'll be all right, Kerry. We'll get her out. I'll get her out. I promise."

Above her head, Jared met Bram's bleak gaze and he knew they were both thinking he'd just made a promise he might not be able to keep.

More than an hour later, the excavation site was littered with fire trucks, emergency vehicles, rescue crews and paramedics. Generators and bright outdoor lights had been set up in preparation for the night to come. The fact that the emergency people anticipated it might take that long to recover Peggy from the pipe tunnel only added to Kerry's worry.

For the umpteenth time, Enola turned a helpless look of frustration on her daughter. "They're wasting time! There's a backhoe sitting right over there. Why don't they start digging her out?"

The two women were standing about thirty feet away from the ditch where Peggy had disappeared. Around them, firemen and other rescue people were discussing ways to bring her daughter out to safety. But Kerry's attention was focused on one lone man rather than the group of professionals. And that one man was Jared Colton.

If anyone could find her daughter and bring her safely out of that mess, it was Jared. She wasn't sure why she'd placed her confidence in him, of all people. She'd never really liked the man. He'd always been a playboy and considered himself God's gift to women. Especially all the sexy sirens around Black Arrow.

It had surprised her enormously to learn he was the man who'd discovered Peggy's whereabouts. She hadn't even known he was still living in Black Arrow. She'd thought he'd moved out years ago and was now making a fortune for some large petroleum company down in Houston.

With unshed tears stinging the back of her eyes, she said quietly, "They have to locate exactly where she is first, Mom. Then maybe they can do something about getting her out."

"Well, I don't know why that Colton boy had to be the one who crawled into the pipe to go searching for her," Enola commented. "He's not a rescue person. He should have let one of the firemen go. Like Tommy Grimes. You remember, he's the one that saved the Wilsons from being blown to smithereens."

Kerry groaned inwardly. Ever since she'd returned to Black Arrow, Tommy had pestered her for a date and she knew her mother had encouraged him simply because he was divorced with a small daughter around Peggy's age.

"If I remember right, the Wilsons' neighbor is the one who discovered propane was leaking inside their house. All Tommy did was turn off the valve at the tank. And as for Jared Colton, he's an engineer, Mom. He's been working on these pipes and he knows all about which way they run and how deep they're buried. I trust him. More than anyone down there.''

Surprised by Kerry's remark, Enola studied her daughter. ''I don't have to tell you he's a rounder, Kerry. The man is in his thirties and he's never been married or had a child of his own. He couldn't know what Peggy means to you or what you're going through right now.''

Normally Enola was an open-minded woman. Kerry couldn't see any reason for her mother to be saying such nasty things about a man who was risking his own life to save her granddaughter's. Unless Enola was simply too upset to know what she was actually saying.

''You're wrong. He does understand. A person doesn't have to be a parent to value a child's life.'' Besides, Kerry thought, she'd heard the caring in his voice when he'd promised her to get Peggy out, felt it for those brief moments when he'd held her against his hard chest. It didn't matter if he was a still a playboy or married with three kids. He was the man she was counting on to save her daughter.

Enola was about to make a reply when a flurry of activity caught Kerry's eye. A mixture of hope and relief flooded through her as she spotted Jared standing at the mouth of the pipe. Although the late afternoon sun was casting long shadows over the group, she could easily see that he was covered with mud. Streaks of it slashed at an angle across his cheek while parts of his short black hair were splotched with brown. In spite of his bedraggled condition, he was wasting no time in relaying information to Bram, and from the quick hand gestures he made back toward the drainpipe, he was a man just starting a mission rather than ending it.

"There's Jared," Kerry said to her mother with a breathless rush. "Maybe he's found Peggy!"

Not waiting to see if her mom was following, Kerry pushed her way through the crowd until she was standing next to Jared and Bram, who'd now been joined by their younger sister, Willow, who ran the Black Arrow Feed and Grain store. There was also Gray, a tall, dark-haired Colton cousin, who was a local judge. Apparently the Colton family believed in banding together in times of crisis, she thought, and in this case she was deeply grateful that their help was being extended to her and Peggy.

Focusing her attention on Jared, she begged, "Tell me. What did you find?"

Jared's gray eyes locked with Kerry's pleading brown gaze. All the while he'd been crawling his way through the maze of drainpipes, his mind had been consumed with thoughts of the agony he knew this woman was going through and of the little girl who must surely be feeling trapped and terrified by now.

Stepping forward, he took her hand and gently folded it between his. "I've located her, Kerry. As I worked my way deeper into the pipe, I kept calling her name. She didn't answer me directly, but I picked up on the sound of her crying."

The relief of hearing that her daughter was alive flooded through Kerry and in the process nearly buckled her knees. If Jared hadn't been holding onto her hand, she would have crumpled right there in the mud.

"Then she must be okay! But—" she stopped abruptly as another thought struck her. "If you could hear her, why didn't you go after her and bring her out?"

He shook his head. "I'm afraid it's not going to be

that simple, Kerry. Your daughter, Peggy—or Bram told me you sometimes call her Chenoa. Which name does she usually go by?''

''Chenoa is her Comanche name which means—''

''Little dove,'' Jared finished for her. One corner of his mouth lifted wryly. ''You must have forgotten that us Coltons are Comanche, too.''

She hadn't forgotten the Coltons, Kerry thought, especially this one. By the time she'd been a senior in high school, he'd had women running out his ears, but for some reason he'd wanted to date her. Back then the idea of going out with a rogue like him was indecent, not to mention unsettling. Even though he'd been incredibly handsome and too sexy for his own good. A fact that hadn't changed as far as she could see.

Flustered that she'd allowed her thoughts to wander, she said, ''My daughter normally goes by Peggy.''

Jared nodded at Kerry while from the corner of his eye he could see that Bram was already talking over a course of action with the rescue people. ''Peggy has wormed her way back into a shaft of pipe that I can't reach,'' he explained to her.

Sick with fear, she gripped his fingers. ''Someone else—someone smaller—'' she began, only to have him dash away her hopeful suggestions with a shake of his head.

''It would take someone smaller than Peggy even. I've found where she'd crawled through to another section of pipe, but her movements disturbed the surrounding ground, causing some of it to cave in behind her. Even if she was smart enough to turn around and find her way back, she couldn't get past the dirt and rocks that are blocking the end of the pipe.''

"Oh God! Oh please tell me you can get her out! Please!"

One of Jared's hands lifted to her shoulder. He gripped it firmly as he looked directly into her eyes. "Kerry, I promise you I'll get her out. I'm not sure exactly how to do it yet, but I'll get her."

Kerry desperately wanted to believe him, but the whole situation sounded so awful. Her baby was in a deep dark hole with no way out. "But she might not have enough air! If it takes a long time to get her out—"

"Now, Kerry, don't panic. If you collapse you won't be much good to Peggy once we do bring her up."

Tears were blurring her eyes and she blinked furiously to prevent them from spilling onto her cheeks. God knew she had a good reason to fall apart, but over the past few years, she'd had to battle her way through tough times. The experiences had taught her to steel herself against personal pain and anguish, to show a brave face even though her heart was breaking. That was the strong, Comanche way, and she wanted Jared Colton to see that she was no weaker than he.

"You're right, Jared," She drew in a bracing breath and squared her shoulders. "What can I do to help?"

Jared glanced up the sloping ground to where Kerry's mother was waiting with a group of people that had grown to large proportions in the past hour. "Just go back to your family and wait. We'll take care of everything." He looked down at her as another notion suddenly struck him. "Wait—there is something. If your husband is here, he could be a help. If he'd be willing to crawl down into the pipe and call to Peggy, she might respond to him. That would help us pinpoint her exact location."

Bitter regret twisted deep in Kerry's stomach. Damon wouldn't be willing to send Peggy a birthday card, much less risk his life to save hers. She tried to swallow away the guilt and sorrow that she felt, not for herself, but for her innocent daughter.

"Uh, he's…not around. But I could crawl into the pipe and call to Peggy," she quickly suggested.

Jared shook his head. "It's too deep and dangerous, Kerry. I don't want to put you at risk."

Her heart sank. "Oh well," she said huskily. "Then I'm—uh, sorry, Jared. Because Peggy doesn't have a father."

Chapter Two

The next few hours were some of the hardest Jared had ever endured. For the sake of the little dove trapped beneath the ground, he was trying to focus all his mental ability on the rescue operation. Yet there was a small part of his thoughts that continually strayed to Kerry.

To learn that she was a single mother had knocked him for a loop. The Kerry WindWalker he remembered was the quiet, reserved waitress who'd worked seven or eight years ago at Woody's Café. At that time he'd tried to get to know her personally, but she'd stubbornly kept the conversation between them to the same light exchange she used for all the customers in the homey little eating place. She'd had a reputation for being prim and proper and, in spite of Jared's best efforts, she'd left Black Arrow with that same squeaky-clean standing.

Jared could only suppose that the years away from Black Arrow had changed her. Although there was one thing that remained the same, he thought ruefully. She had no man in her life. The fact that she'd been raising her daughter alone saddened him. Yet he had to confess there was a selfish part of him that was glad she wasn't attached to some other man.

"Okay, Jared, that's ten feet. Want me to go any deeper?"

Shaking away his thoughts, Jared looked up at Newt, a burly oilfield worker who was operating a large auger. This was the second hole that had been drilled into the ground near to the spot where Peggy was trapped. The first had failed to give Jared an entrance to reach her. After a long, careful study from inside the ground, coupled with the engineering blueprints he had of the original layout of the drainage pipes, he'd finally decided to try another, at a closer angle.

"No. That's good. Hop out, Newt, and I'll go down. Maybe this one will get me all the way back to her."

Someone caught him by the arm and Jared glanced around to find Bram at his side. Having his brother here for support, even in the capacity of sheriff, helped him forget that he'd been at this for hours and that his body was now running on sheer adrenaline.

"Newt has reached the right depth," he quickly explained to Bram. "I'm going down again."

"What if you can't get through this time, Jared?"

"I've got to," Jared said grimly. "I'm afraid to drill any closer. From what I know about this network of pipes, Peggy probably has some space to crawl back and forth. I can't risk drilling into an area where she might be."

Bram let out a weary breath. "I know you're right.

But she's been down there for hours now. The tunnel you've just now bored may not be any better than the last one.''

The desperation in Bram's voice matched the feelings that Jared had been dealing with from the moment he'd spotted Peggy's little footprints. He wouldn't rest until that child was placed safely in her mother's arms.

Jared lifted the hard hat from his sweaty head and shoved a weary hand through his damp hair. ''Believe me, brother, I want to get her out just as badly as you do. So have a little confidence in me, will you? This time I'll get in. I have to,'' he said with steely determination. Glancing back over his shoulder, he scanned the crowd that had continued to grow throughout the evening. ''Have you seen Kerry?''

''I talked to her about ten minutes ago. I explained that you were drilling again at another angle.''

''How was she doing?''

Bram's tight grimace spoke volumes. ''She's holding herself together, but it's pretty obvious she's not far from collapsing. Her mother tells me that no one has been able to make her eat or drink anything since we've been out here.''

Just the thought of what she must be going through was enough to make Jared sick. ''See what you and Gray can do with her,'' Jared told him. ''I'm going down. And I'm not coming up until I have Peggy with me. Even if it means I have to dig her out by hand!''

By now Newt had removed the steel auger from the newly drilled hole. Jared hurried toward the open cavity. Bram followed to snatch a hold on Jared's shoulder before he could lower himself into the newly bored hole.

''Jared, you're exhausted,'' he pointed out. ''You've

already worked for hours. Let someone else go down. Let me. Or Gray.''

Shaking his head at his older brother's plea, Jared said, ''You're the sheriff. You need to be out here where you can make sure everyone is safe and doing what they're supposed to be doing. This town would be in chaos if it lost you.''

Jared's offhand compliment put a twisted smile on Bram's face. ''This town survived a long time before I became sheriff and it'll go on surviving once I'm no longer in office. But that's not the issue. You're about to fall over and Gray—''

''Doesn't like to get his hands dirty,'' Jared joked and winked. Then before Bram could try to dissuade him any further, he lowered himself into the ground.

Kerry was trying her best not to keep glancing at the small watch on her wrist, but each minute seemed to be crawling by as she and the rest of the hundred or more people around the excavation site waited for Jared to reappear and prayed that Peggy would be in his arms.

''Kerry, is there anything I can get for you? A sandwich? Or cold drink?''

Kerry looked around to see Christa, a co-worker at Liberty Bank, who'd also become a good friend. The tall, curvaceous blonde was two years younger than Kerry and had already gone through a traumatic divorce. Over the past months Kerry had been trying to help her young friend get through the trying ordeal. Now the tables were turned and Christa was here to lend Kerry what support she could.

Trying to smile, Kerry passed trembling fingers

across her forehead. "No thanks, Christa. I tried to eat earlier, but everything just stuck in my throat."

With a worried frown, Christa grabbed a folding portable stool that one of the local churches had distributed for the crowd. Once she was sitting next to her friend, she said, "Clarence told me that you worked through lunch. It's nearly eight o'clock now. You have to be starving."

Kerry placed a reassuring hand over Christa's. "I'm fine. Or at least I will be once they get Peggy out of there." Closing her eyes, she swallowed at the knot of fear that had lodged in her throat and refused to go away.

"I noticed the sheriff was talking to you a few minutes ago," Christa remarked. "What was he saying? Does he know anything yet?"

"He said that the phone Jared had taken with him had apparently quit working. They haven't been able to make any contact with him in the past twenty minutes."

Christa shook her head. "Well, that doesn't necessarily mean that something has gone wrong. The battery could have gone dead on the phone or the signal may not be getting out."

Opening her eyes, Kerry focused a desperate look on her friend. "I hope you're right, Christa. I can't—I have to think that things are going to be okay. Otherwise—" She couldn't go on as tears trickled onto her cheeks. Moments later, she felt Christa's hand gently patting her back. Sniffing, she wiped at her tears and tried again, "Oh Christa—I don't know what I'd do if I lost my daughter."

"You're not going to lose her," Christa said with firm resolution. "The Coltons will see to that. They're a smart, diligent family. And they care about people. If Jared can't get her out, he and his brother will call in some expert who can.''

Kerry glanced around her to make sure her mother wasn't within earshot. ''I'm glad to hear you say that,'' she said in a voice only Christa could hear. ''Mom keeps preaching that they're making a mess out of things and just wanting to big-shot around and take over the situation.''

A puzzled expression came over Christa's face. ''I can't understand that. Let's face it, the fire and rescue people in this town mean well and they do a good job most of the time, but they're not that highly trained. They have no idea what's under this ground or how to get into it without tearing everything apart and endangering Peggy even more. Jared's an engineer. He knows what he's dealing with.''

Kerry let out a long, shaky breath. ''That's what I was thinking, but Mom seems to have something against Jared in particular.''

Christa shrugged. ''Well, from what I've heard, he used to have quite a reputation with the ladies. Your mom probably holds that against him.''

Shaking her head with weary disbelief, Kerry said, ''That has nothing to do with him getting my daughter out of the ground! I don't understand her—''

''Kerry! Look!''

Christa's abrupt cry was coupled with a ripple of excitement passing through the people gathered around the site. And then Kerry saw the reason for all the commotion. It was Jared! He was climbing out of the deep ditch and Peggy was nestled safely in his arms!

Choking back a sob of sheer relief, Kerry jumped to

her feet and stumbled across the rough ground to meet them.

"Peggy! Oh baby!" she cried, not bothering to hide the tears of joy that were beginning to stream down her face.

Jared grinned down at her. "Your daughter is a little muddy and dirty, but other than that she seems to be okay," he said.

From the moment he'd reached Peggy back in the narrow cavern of pipe, she'd had a death grip on his neck. Even now, with her mother near, she was reluctant to loosen her hold and allow him to place her in Kerry's arms.

Gently, Jared patted the child's back, then carefully pushed the long tangle of black hair from the side of her face. "It's all right, Chenoa," he murmured to the frightened little girl. "Your mommy is right here. She's been waiting for you. Just like I promised."

Kerry swallowed down her tears in an effort to make her voice sound as calm and normal as possible to her daughter. "Peggy, it's all right, honey. You can come to mama now and we'll go get Fred."

Lifting her face from Jared's wide shoulder, Peggy looked warily around her, then down at Kerry's outstretched arms.

"Mama," she said through sniffles and hiccups, then reached for her mother.

Jared had accomplished a few difficult jobs down through the years, jobs that had left him feeling proud, maybe even a little smug. But he could truthfully say nothing he'd ever done felt as wonderful or satisfying as being able to place Peggy into her mother's arms. And the elated smile that was now spreading across

Kerry's face was worth every minute he'd spent crawling through that muddy underground maze.

Hugging her daughter fiercely to her breast, Kerry looked up at Jared. She was unaware of the crowd surging around them, nor did she hear their cheers of joy. There was only him and her and the precious feeling of her daughter's arms clinging tightly to her neck.

"Thank you, Jared. Thank you from the bottom of my heart."

The raw emotion in her trembling words humbled him, touched him in a spot he hadn't known he possessed.

"There's no need for you to thank me, Kerry. I wanted to get Peggy out of there as much as you wanted to have her back."

Shifting Peggy's weight to one arm, Kerry extended her hand to Jared. He folded his fingers around hers with a firm reassuring grip. As their hands warmed together, he realized the past horrific hours had connected him to this woman in an oddly intimate way. Even now he could feel her relief and joy in the same way he'd felt her earlier desperation and fear.

"I'll never forget what you've done for me," she said to him "And when Peggy gets old enough to understand, I'll explain to her that a very brave man saved her life."

Jared was like most any red-blooded male from eighteen months old to eighty. He liked to show off for any appreciative female, maybe even preen a little bit if the occasion warranted. But tonight was a different situation. And he didn't want this woman to get the impression that he was hero material. He wasn't. He was just a man who wouldn't give up until the job was done.

"Not brave, Kerry. Just stubborn," he corrected.

Her eyes still wet with grateful tears, she raised up on tiptoe and kissed his dirty cheek. "Then thank you for being a stubborn man, Jared Colton."

"Kerry! Is Peggy all right? Is there anything broken?"

Stunned by the brief, intimate contact, Jared watched Kerry turn away to answer Enola's frantic question. Moments later, he felt a nudge in his rib cage and looked around to see that he was now bracketed by a grinning brother and cousin.

Gray, who was only a year younger than Jared, said, "Well old cousin, looks like you're certainly the hero at this little gathering."

His description of the crowd around them as "a little gathering" was quite an understatement. It seemed like half the townsfolk were swarming around them like bees.

Jared slipped off his hard hat. The night breeze felt cool against his sweating head. Pushing his fingers through his wet hair, he said to Gray, "Hell, I didn't do anything but crawl into a hole."

Bram punched him affectionately in the shoulder and chuckled. "Looks to me like Kerry WindWalker thought you did more than that."

Jared glanced back around to see that she and her young daughter had been swallowed up by the crowd. It was just as well, he thought.

"The only thing you saw was a woman grateful to get her daughter back," Jared said, aiming the statement at both his brother and cousin.

Bram was about to make another comment on the subject when one of his deputies approached with a question for his boss. The moment Bram turned his attention to the deputy, Jared used the opportunity to make his own escape.

"I'm going home," he told Gray. "Tell Bram I'll deal with getting some of this heavy equipment back to its rightful owners."

Gray slung his arm around Jared's shoulders. "Will do," he assured him. "You go get some rest."

"Yeah. I'll talk to you tomorrow," Jared told him.

As Jared slipped through the crowd, several people called out to him, a few even stopped him to shake his hand, pat his back and offer him congratulations on a job well done.

Normally, Jared would have hung around and lapped up all the attention and praise. It wasn't often a man was handed the chance to do something as meaningful and worthwhile as saving a child's life. And it warmed him that people appreciated his efforts. Yet he didn't linger in the crowd. Instead he continued toward the quiet, dark spot where his truck was parked.

By the time Jared climbed into the vehicle, bone-weary exhaustion had overtaken him. He drew in a string of long breaths, then rested his forehead against the steering wheel for several moments before he finally started the motor.

As he pulled away from the scene, he glanced toward the activity still going on around the excavation site. Rescue workers were already starting to move away the fire trucks and other recovery vehicles which had been needed during the long hours. Some yards away from the commotion, he spotted Kerry at the back of an ambulance with Peggy in her arms and talking happily to Jenna Elliot.

Thirty minutes later as Jared fell into bed, he was still holding that happy image in his mind.

* * *

Kerry waited patiently at the back of an ambulance while a petite, blond-haired, blue-eyed nurse named Jenna Elliot checked Peggy over for any sign of injuries.

Kerry had never met Jenna before, but she knew of her family. Her father was a powerful businessman and politician in Black Arrow, and though corruption had been linked to his name, he was still an influential man. However, from the moment Kerry had walked up to the ambulance with Peggy, Jenna had seemed sincerely compassionate and caring. She also seemed to be casting more than a few furtive glances at Sheriff Bram Colton, too.

"Your daughter seems to be perfectly fine," Jenna said to Kerry as she handed Peggy back to her. "However, if it would make you feel at ease you could have her pediatrician check her over, too. But I'm sure you don't have any worries. She seems like a very healthy little girl."

"And very adventurous," Kerry added jokingly. And she could joke now, thanks to Jared Colton, she thought as she turned to go home, clutching a sleepy Peggy in her arms.

Jared Colton. Of all the men in Black Arrow, Kerry wouldn't have thought of him as a hero. Eight years ago, before she'd left for Virginia, he'd been a frequent diner at Woody's Café where she'd worked as a waitress on the evening shift. For a man that was part Comanche, he'd done a lot of talking. Most of it directed at the adoring females who'd always seemed to flock around him. But Kerry hadn't forgotten the small part of his glib tongue that had been aimed at her.

For the most part, Kerry had tried to keep the conversation between them cool and impersonal, but there had been times she'd felt him looking at her in the same way a red-tailed hawk would look at a juicy little field mouse. On those occasions she'd always scurried back to the kitchen, her head down so that no one might see the scarlet color stinging her cheeks. No man had ever made her feel so naked and vulnerable. And eight years later she could safely say that hadn't changed. He still left her breathless and rattled.

"Kerry? Are you listening?"

At the sound of Enola's voice, Kerry pulled her eyes away from a nearby open window and looked up to see her mother standing at the entryway to the small living room of the WindWalker home.

"Sorry, Mom. I was—lost in thought. Were you asking me something?"

Her forehead furrowed with a frown, Enola stepped into the room. A dishtowel was twisted between her hardworking hands.

"I was wondering if we should wake Peggy for supper. She hasn't eaten hardly anything today. With everything that happened yesterday, she should get something in her tummy."

"I know. But I think she needs to rest more."

Enola moved closer to her daughter. "She's been like a different little girl today. I doubt she's said twenty words altogether. I couldn't even get her to help me dig in the garden."

Kerry didn't need to be reminded that Peggy was still suffering emotionally from the horrible experience she'd gone through. Her daughter had hardly left her side all day. And though the paramedics had found her physically unharmed, Kerry realized her daughter had been traumatized.

"She just needs time to get over this, Mom. We all do."

Enola briefly closed her eyes and Kerry realized her mother was still trying to deal with the guilt she felt over allowing Peggy to slip away unnoticed.

Rising from her chair, Kerry patted her mother's shoulder. "I wish you would quit blaming yourself, Mom. None of this is your fault. Peggy has pulled disappearing acts on me before. It just so happened that this time she wandered farther off than she'd intended."

Enola sighed. "She's only three, Kerry. She doesn't understand the dangers. She wants to see everything. Learn about everything. I should have known not to turn my back. Even for a second."

Kerry shook her head. "Mom, that's ridiculous. No child can be watched that closely. And maybe in the long run, this horrible experience has taught her not to stray from the house or yard."

"I hope you're right. But it's heartbreaking to see my granddaughter so quiet and withdrawn."

Looping her arm through her mother's, she urged her toward the kitchen. "Peggy is brave. Like her grandmother and great-grandmother Crow. She'll get through this. Now come on and let's eat."

The two women made their way back to the small kitchen where Enola had prepared pinto beans, corn bread and wilted salad. Inside the room, they were greeted with the aroma of cooked food joined by the scents of cut grass and sweet lilac wafting through the open screen door.

While her mother took a seat at the dining table, Kerry went to the cabinet to fill two tall glasses with iced tea. When a knock sounded at the front of the house, the two women exchanged glances.

"I'll go see who it is," Kerry said to Enola. "You go ahead and eat. It's probably just another neighbor wanting to make sure Peggy is okay."

Not bothering to hunt for her shoes, Kerry padded barefoot over the cool linoleum until she reached the front screen door. Since no one was standing directly in view, she pushed it open and stepped onto the porch.

"Hello Kerry."

The deep voice hit her before she spotted him standing at the south end of the porch. Slowly she turned to see the man who had continued to linger in her thoughts today.

"Hello," she said quietly as he walked toward her.

Although he was dressed casually in jeans and boots and a pale blue polo shirt, she felt sloppy in comparison. Her white shorts were stained with tiny splotches of blue paint and the red T-shirt topping them had been washed so many times it had turned the color of a half-ripe watermelon. Greeting her neighbors in such a getup was one thing, but letting Jared Colton catch her like this was quite another.

"I hope I'm not interrupting anything," he said as his eyes roamed appreciatively over her face, then lowered to her bare brown legs. "I just happened to be in the neighborhood this evening and I thought I'd check to see how Peggy is doing."

There it was again, Kerry thought, that strange feeling of being exposed in front of this man. What was it about him, she wondered. She'd been around nice-looking men before. But none of them had affected her like this one. Not even Peggy's father.

His dark bronze features were rough-hewn, but classic male. The strong, hawkish nose, carved cheekbones and black hair edging over the back of his collar were distinctly Native American. Only his gray eyes and the faint shadow of a beard hinted that there might be white blood flowing through his veins.

She tried not to stare at his striking face or the long, strong body attached to it as she replied, "We were about to eat supper. Peggy is asleep right now. But you're welcome to join us."

Kerry was trying to be polite, but Jared could see that the last thing she wanted him to do was join her and her mother for supper. The fact left him feeling vaguely hollow. Though he didn't understand why. There were plenty of women in town that would be thrilled to find him on their front steps. Once he left here all he had to do was pick up his cell phone and make a call to one of them. And maybe he'd do that, he promised himself. It was foolish to let this single mother change his normal behavior.

Giving her his best smile, he shook his head. "Thank you, Kerry, but I wouldn't want to impose."

Disappointment flashed through her, catching her completely off guard. She didn't want to entertain this man, she silently argued with herself. It would be like inviting a stick of dynamite into the house. And she'd already had too many explosions in her life to risk another one.

Feeling incredibly awkward, she tucked her bobbed hair behind her ears and darted a glance toward his face. "I hope you've had a chance to get rested up from yesterday's ordeal," she said.

He shrugged as though the part he'd played in Peggy's rescue had been superfluous. Kerry could only wonder if the gesture was an attempt to appear humble or if these past years had honestly changed him into a more modest man than the Jared Colton she remembered.

"I'm fine," he said with a quick grin. "What about you? How are you holding up?"

It was a beautiful spring evening. The sun had dipped below the bare hills that skirted the edge of town and a warm breeze was blowing the scent of honeysuckle across the porch. If this man had been anyone except Jared Colton she might have enjoyed having male company for a change. She might have invited him to take a seat and drink a glass of tea with her. Instead, she was afraid to trust him and afraid to trust herself.

"I'm okay. It's Peggy and Mom that worry me. Peggy is—well, she's hardly spoken to anyone today. And she's eaten even less than she's talked. Mother blames herself, of course. I'm not sure how to help either one of them."

"I hate to hear that. I was hoping Peggy would be the sort of child that would bounce right back." A rueful grin suddenly twisted his lips. "I mean, there's not many little girls her age that would have enough courage to go exploring a deep dark place like she went into. Especially without another child with her."

His remarks surprised Kerry. She'd not expected him to understand anything about the way a child's mind worked. Especially a little female mind. But then females were his specialty; he ought to know how their minds worked, she quickly reminded herself.

"Peggy is very adventurous. I used to be proud of the fact that she was so curious about the world around her. But now I'm wondering if that curiosity is a curse. When I asked her why she left the yard, she told me that she went hunting birds with Fred. I don't even know if she understands what the term hunting means. No one that I know of has talked about hunting birds or anything else to her.''

She looked weary, Jared thought. The harrowing hours she'd gone through yesterday and last night would have been enough to break any young mother. Much less one without the support of a husband. And suddenly he wished he had the right to try to comfort her with touches and whispered words.

''She's probably heard someone refer to Fred as a hunting dog,'' Jared suggested. ''Or it could have come from television.''

Kerry nodded. ''You could be right. Either way, I'm wondering now how to keep this from happening again. I don't want to get rid of the dog. Losing her buddy would only make matters worse.''

His black brows pulled together in a thoughtful frown. ''I don't have any kids, Kerry, so I'm the last person to give you advice. But I used to be a kid with a dog and I know losing him would have broken my heart.''

Hearing one of Black Arrow's most prominent playboys discuss children and dogs and broken hearts was as unsettling to Kerry as the potent sensuality that swirled around him. Because it made him more of a man somehow. A man that she could care about.

Alarmed by the soft thoughts running through her head, she glanced away from him and breathed deeply. ''I'm—uh—I've been thinking I'll go by the animal shelter and adopt a kitty for her, too. That way if Fred decides to take off again, she might decide it's more important for her to stay behind and take care of her new friend.''

A grin lifted the corner of his lips, giving her a glimpse of snow-white teeth. "That sounds like a great idea. As long as Fred doesn't decide he wants to make a meal out of the cat."

Kerry actually laughed and the unexpected sound darted through Jared like a ray of golden sunshine. Of all the times he'd been in her presence he'd never heard her laugh before. It made him wonder if the years had loosened her rigid personality or if she was just now allowing him to see the woman she'd always been.

"I'm not too worried about that," she said. "He loves all of our neighboring felines."

Enola's voice suddenly carried through the screen door. "Kerry? Who is it?"

Both Kerry and Jared turned to see Enola stepping onto the porch with a sleepy-eyed Peggy in her arms.

"Jared has stopped by to check on Peggy," Kerry quickly explained to her mother. "I asked him to join us for supper—but he has other plans."

"Good evening, Mrs. WindWalker," Jared greeted the older woman.

She inclined her head in his direction but didn't grant him any sort of semblance of a smile. Jared couldn't help notice the woman's eagle-eyed gaze was encompassing both him and her daughter as though she was trying to gauge the sort of conversation that had been going on before she'd arrived. Her attitude was faintly insulting, but Jared tried his best to ignore it. From what he knew of Marvin WindWalker, it wouldn't surprise him if Enola despised all men.

"Evening," she stiffly replied.

Jared's attention zeroed in on Peggy, who was chewing on one finger while studying him with guarded interest.

Stepping closer, he smiled at the little girl. "Hello Peggy. Do you remember me?"

Peggy squirmed in Enola's arms and demanded to be put down. Then to her mother and grandmother's total surprise, she scurried across the wooden porch straight to Jared.

"You're Jared," she said, then held up her arms to him in a totally trustful gesture.

A rush of tender emotions filled his chest as Jared bent down and scooped up the child. After carefully balancing her with one arm against his chest, he touched a forefinger to her cheek.

"That's right, little dove. I'm Jared."

Peggy's tiny fingers reached out and played with his shirt collar, a signal, Jared realized, that she felt comfortable with him.

"You got me out of that hole," she said to him.

Jared was surprised at her clearly pronounced words. Last night she'd refused to say anything to him except that she wanted her mama. And those words had been muffled with tears.

"That's right, sweetheart. And I'm glad I did. You're just about the prettiest little girl I've ever seen."

For a moment her lips twitched as though she might give him a smile. Then all of a sudden she threw her arms around his neck and held on tight. Since fathering skills were something Jared knew precious little about, all he could do was follow his instincts and pat Peggy's back with gentle reassurance.

A few steps away, Kerry tried to swallow away the tightness in her throat as she watched her daughter's reaction to Jared. Even though Peggy was usually a tiny tornado, she'd always been slow to warm up to the male gender. To see her clinging so trustingly to Jared, a man she'd only seen once, was somewhat of a phenomenon.

Across the porch, Enola cleared her throat loudly. "Peggy, it's time for you to eat supper," she said firmly. "Tell Mr. Colton goodbye."

Peggy ignored her grandmother and continued to bury her face against Jared's neck. At the same time, Kerry stared with an open mouth at her mother.

She gathered her wits and said, "Mom, I'll handle this. Why don't you go finish eating. We'll join you in a few minutes."

The surprise that registered on Enola's face told Jared the older woman wasn't accustomed to having Kerry intercede with her own wishes. Especially in such a blunt way. Enola opened her mouth to say something else. But instead, she threw Jared a withering look, then turned and headed into the house.

Once the woman was out of sight, Jared joked in an effort to lighten the moment, "I don't think she likes me."

Kerry sighed. "Her behavior embarrasses me. I don't know what's making her this way."

Jared did. There weren't many mothers in Black Arrow that welcomed the sight of him on the doorstep. He knew he had a reputation for dallying with women's hearts, maybe even crushing a few. If that was true, he'd not done it intentionally. Of all the women he'd dated in the past, he'd never once led them to believe he was a serious suitor with marriage on his mind. They'd gone into a relationship with him knowing it would only be fun and games. But convincing Enola WindWalker of that would be as fruitless as talking to the wall.

"Forget it," he told Kerry with a rueful grin. "I take no offense. Especially since I got such a nice greeting from my little dove here." Placing his forefinger under Peggy's chin, he lifted the angelic face up to his. "Are you going to be a good girl for your mother and stay in the yard from now on?"

Peggy nodded emphatically and Jared stroked the shiny black waves tumbling about her shoulders. He could see touches of Kerry in the girl's proud thin nose, high cheekbones and faintly pointed chin. Yet her café au lait complexion made Jared suspect her father had been a white man. His own father had been half-white.

"That's just what I wanted to hear," he told her proudly.

"I have a dog," Peggy said to him. "Do you have a dog?"

Jared chuckled as he found himself charmed by a set of big brown eyes and twin dimples. "No. But I met your Mr. Fred yesterday. And you know what, I think he's almost as smart as you are."

Peggy gave him another emphatic nod of agreement, then to Kerry and Jared's amazement, she leaned forward and smacked a kiss on his cheek.

"I gotta go feed Fred," she said suddenly, then squirmed, signaling that she wanted to be put back on her feet.

Jared complied, and smiled as he watched her scurry into the house.

"Looks like I need to be thanking you again," Kerry said.

He turned his head in her direction and was instantly taken with the natural beauty of her face, the sensual curves, partially camouflaged by her loose clothing. She was not a glamour girl. So why did he wonder, as he had so many years ago, what she would look like in his arms with nothing on but a smile just for him?

"For what?" he asked, forcing his mind off the tempting thought.

"That's the most Peggy has said to anyone today. She's obviously taken with you."

Jared was glad the child had warmed up to him. Yet it was her mother that he really wanted to charm.

Shrugging, he glanced down at the toe of his boot and wondered why this woman made him feel like a shy teenager wanting to steal a kiss. "Well, I'm kinda taken with her, too. That's why I wanted to stop by and check on her."

Kerry folded her hands primly in front of her. "Thank you. It was kind of you."

No, it was selfish, Jared thought. Sure, he'd wanted to see little Peggy and make sure she was okay. But even more he'd wanted to see this woman. Yet he wasn't going to confess such a thing to her. Right now she saw him as a gallant knight and he didn't want to spoil it.

With a sudden grin, he lifted a hand in farewell. "You'd better go get your supper, Kerry. Before your mama comes after you."

Kerry watched him walk to his truck. As he pulled away from the house, she wondered if this was the last time she would ever see him. Or if Jared Colton was going to try to make her one more notch on the foot of his bed.

Chapter Three

The kitten's meow was more like a squall of protest. Jared glanced down at the small animal carrier sitting on the truck seat beside him. The yellow tabby had caught his eye the first moment the volunteer worker at the shelter had shown him into the room of orphaned cats. His broad nose, proud tail and coarse voice had convinced Jared he would be the perfect companion to frisky Fred and Peggy.

"Just hold on and I'll let you out of that cage," he told the cat as he turned off the main highway and onto a graveled dirt road.

At the end of the dusty, quarter-mile drive, stood an old square ranch house with a hip roof and a porch bordering three sides. The house and two acres had come up for rent five years ago when a local farmer had sold off the surrounding crop land and moved into town. Jared had taken it on a long-term lease, mainly to have a place to hang his hat when work brought him back to the Black Arrow vicinity.

There were times the old house stood empty for months running. But Jared had never had a problem with stealing or vandalism. There were benefits to having the county sheriff as your brother, he thought with great affection. Also to having a sister who was kind enough to keep the dust from piling up inside. And from the looks of the pickup truck parked to one side of the driveway, Willow must have taken pity on him and stopped by today to do a little cleaning.

After parking the truck in front of a faded wooden fence that separated the yard from weedy pasture, Jared climbed out and carefully carried the caged cat into the house. The moment he closed the door behind him, he was hit by the smell of fresh-baked cookies and the sound of his sister's voice. He followed the sound into the kitchen to see her sitting on the tall barstool he kept beneath the wall phone.

"Here he is now," she said to the caller. "So I'll let you ask him."

Jared cocked a questioning brow at her. She mouthed the word "newspaper" as she handed him the phone.

Two minutes later, Jared hung up.

"That was quick," Willow remarked.

"I'm sure he'd already told you that he wanted to do an interview with me, Kerry and Peggy. I told him we'd meet him here tomorrow night." He made a general wave in the direction of the sink full of dirty dishes. "Do you think you could clean the place up a bit?"

Willow shook her head in amazement. "Listen, little brother, you might not even need this place cleaned up when Kerry hears that you didn't bother to consult her about this meeting. Sounds to me like you're asking for big trouble.''

He probably was asking for trouble, Jared thought, but not the sort his sister had in mind. "I'll get her to agree," he told her with a confident grin, then motioned for her to follow him out to the living room. "Come here and look what I've got."

"What is this?" Willow exclaimed as soon as she spotted the animal cage sitting in the middle of the floor. "You found a snake at the work site?"

He chuckled. "I'm not into reptiles. I like soft, cuddly things."

"Hmm, don't I know it," she said dryly.

Jared bent down and unlatched the cage. The tabby pranced out as if he was ready to take possession of the place.

Willow squealed with pleasure, then quickly knelt down and stroked the cat's arched back. "Oh, how adorable! Where did he come from?"

"I stopped by the animal shelter on my way home."

His black-haired, gray-eyed sister looked up at him with disbelief. "Am I hearing this right? My playboy brother actually adopted a kitten? What are you going to do with him when your job here is finished? Take him with you?"

Jared laughed at her flurry of questions. "He's not for me. He's a gift to Peggy WindWalker. Her mother thought it would be a good idea to get her a kitten, so that she wouldn't be tempted to follow her dog away from the house."

Willow smiled at the kitten as he batted at a piece of fuzz he'd discovered under the edge of an armchair. "So you took it upon yourself to get the kitten for her," she said with sudden understanding.

Grinning, Jared bent down and picked up the kitten. "The last time I looked it wasn't against the law to give someone a gift."

Willow laughed again. "Little Peggy must have made quite an impression on you. I can't ever remember you taking such an interest in a child." She slanted him a knowing look. "Or is it her mother that's the real appeal here?"

Jared chuckled as he rubbed the yellow tom between the ears. "Wouldn't you like to know."

Willow clucked her tongue in disapproval. "Jared, I can tell you right now that you're headed in the wrong direction. Kerry WindWalker is not your style."

Nestling the cat against his chest, Jared headed out of the room. "And how would you know my style?" he tossed over his shoulder.

Willow followed her brother into the kitchen. "Probably because I've watched you go from one pretty face to another these past ten years. You like easy, fun-loving women who have reputations for being just as reckless as yourself. Kerry seems like she's the complete opposite. As far as I know she's a nice girl. You'd be bored to death."

He poured a small amount of milk onto a saucer then placed it and the cat on the floor. "Maybe I'm getting tired of reckless, fun-loving girls."

Willow rolled her eyes. "That'll be the day."

Jared feigned an offended look. "I do have my serious moments, sis. Besides, I'm only asking her to do an interview, not spend the rest of her life with me."

An hour later, Jared parked in front of the Wind-Walker house and carried the cat, cage and all to the front porch. A tight-lipped Enola met him at the door and Jared decided a door-to-door salesman would have probably been greeted with more enthusiasm.

"Hello Mrs. WindWalker. Is Kerry home?"

"She's eating supper right now. Maybe you'd better come back some other time."

Clearly the woman didn't want him around. But Kerry was a grown woman with a child of her own. If Jared was going to be kicked off the place, he wanted Kerry to do it herself. Not her smothering mother.

"I'll just wait out here until she finishes," Jared told her.

Not bothering to wait for the woman's reply, he took a seat on the end of the porch and placed the cat cage beside him. After a few moments he heard the low murmur of voices, then the sound of the front screen opening and closing.

Glancing over his shoulder, he saw Kerry bearing down on him and she wasn't exactly smiling.

"What are you doing here?" she asked without preamble.

Jared stood and gave her a wide grin. "I brought Peggy a gift. Is she here?"

Kerry's eyes darted to the animal cage. Before she could ask, Jared said, "It's a kitty. Come look."

Kerry couldn't believe he was here. Again. And she certainly couldn't believe he'd brought a kitten with him. The whole picture was sending up warning flags right and left.

"Jared, when I tossed the idea to you about Peggy having a cat, it wasn't my intention for you to bring her one."

"Yeah, I know. But I wanted to do this for Peggy." He opened the cage and allowed the little yellow tomcat to venture onto the porch.

Rather than squeal with delight like his sister had done, Kerry stared stonily down at the cat as he rubbed himself against her bare legs.

"Don't you think he's cute?" Jared prompted.

"All kittens are cute," she said, trying her best not to be sucked into his playful attitude. Perhaps he had truly wanted to give Peggy a gift, she thought. But something was warning her that this man would use any and every means available to get what he wanted. If his wants included her, then Kerry was going to have to set him straight. She wasn't available to him.

Jared picked up the kitten and scratched him behind the ears. "Kerry, loosen up. There's no strings attached to this little animal."

The idea that he'd read her thoughts flooded Kerry's face with embarrassed heat. Jared Colton could have most any woman he set his steel-gray eyes on. She was putting herself on a pedestal to think he was interested in her.

"I wasn't thinking that," she quickly denied. "It's just that I wanted to choose the pet I thought would fit my daughter."

Pleased that she was softening, he said, "Well, just look at this little guy. He's perfect."

Kerry pretended to study the cat's autocratic face, but in actuality her eyes were begging to slip up to Jared's strong, sensual features. Like yesterday, she'd spent most of her time today trying not to think about this man. So far she'd failed and his showing up on the doorstep once again had literally been like a cherry topping off a sinful ice cream sundae.

"I think Peggy—"

Her words were suddenly interrupted by the slam of the screen door. Both Kerry and Jared turned to see

Peggy standing on the porch, studying the two of them with quiet interest. She was dressed in sturdy striped overalls and a red T-shirt. Her shiny black hair was fastened in ponytails behind each ear and Jared couldn't help thinking that next to her mother, she was the most adorable little thing he'd ever seen.

Just looking at the child made Jared wonder, as he had many times these past few days, how any man could have given up his own child. Or maybe he was jumping to conclusions about things he didn't know about, Jared thought. It could be that Peggy's father was still somewhere in the background. Perhaps seeing her on an odd weekend or taking her for a couple of weeks in the summer, sending her birthday cards and telephone calls. Yet Jared seriously doubted that was the case. If a man cared enough about his child to do that much, then he surely would have shown up when she was trapped beneath the ground.

Peggy doesn't have a daddy. Kerry's words had pretty much said it all.

"Hi Peggy," he said, then, not waiting for her to come to him, he went over and knelt down to her height. "Did you finish eating your supper?"

She nodded as her fascinated gaze vacillated between his face and the kitten he was holding. "You have a kitty," she finally spoke.

Jared smiled at her. "That's right. I have a kitty for you."

He placed the animal at Peggy's feet and her eyes slowly lit up like a candle on Christmas Eve.

"Do you like him?"

The answer was a squeal of excitement as she made a dive for the animal. Before she could put a choke hold on the cat's neck, Jared quickly took control and showed her how to hold him gently and carefully. The child listened intently to his instructions and after a few minutes, she was carrying the kitten with the same care as her baby dolls.

"That's my girl," Jared praised her, "now go show your mother."

Peggy raced across the porch to where Kerry had been watching the scene taking place between her daughter and Jared. For years now, she'd longed to give Peggy some sort of male contact to make up for the absence of a father. Yet she'd never found a man she trusted enough to allow him into Peggy's sheltered life. And though she might not trust Jared Colton, it appeared her daughter had already decided to make him her trusty friend.

"Look Mama, Jared brought me a cat," she said proudly. "I'm gonna name him Claws. See, he has claws on his toes. But they don't scratch."

Kerry bent over her daughter and made a show of inspecting the kitten. "He can scratch, Peggy. Just like the neighbor's cat," she warned her. "That's why you must handle him like Jared taught you."

At that moment Fred came bounding around the side of the house. Sensing that something interesting was going on, the dog leaped onto the porch and for the next few minutes, the scene was comical as the dog and cat greeted each other, then decided to be buddies.

When Peggy and the animals finally quieted down and left the porch to play out on the clipped grass, Jared sidled up to Kerry.

"I think she likes him," he said, unable to keep a bit of smugness from his voice. He'd never realized that pleasing a child could make him feel so good.

"Oh, she likes him all right," Kerry said with a sigh of resignation.

Jared darted her a look. "Why do you say it like that? Are you still mad at me?"

The wounded, incredulous tone in his voice made it impossible for Kerry to prevent a grin from spreading across her lips. "Yes, I am. I should make you take that kitten back home with you."

The smile on his face practically oozed confidence. "You couldn't do that to Peggy or to Claws. They've already become fast friends."

He was right and he knew it. Kerry had no choice but to let her daughter keep the kitten.

"It is nice to hear her laugh again," Kerry admitted. "I think that's the first I've heard her laugh since she was lost in the pipe."

"I'm glad," he said, then taking her by the shoulder he urged her to take a seat on the edge of the porch. "Sit down here beside me. I have something to ask you."

Kerry was instantly on guard as she kept her bare thigh a respectable distance from his. "Couldn't this question have been asked standing up?" she replied.

He grinned. "Sure. But this is much nicer like this."

For him maybe. For her it was more than a little disconcerting. Her heart was a quick drum beat in her chest. Her breathing seemed to be going in and out too quickly to satisfy her lungs.

"Okay," she said, hoping she sounded normal. "What is this question?"

Her hands were folded together atop her lap. As Jared angled his body around to hers, his first instinct was to reach for one of them. But he quickly decided not to push his luck. Two nights ago while Peggy had been trapped in the drainpipe, he'd had a good excuse to touch her in a comforting way. But this evening they were simply a man and a woman.

"Well, I—when I got home this evening from work, the local newspaper was on the phone with my sister. Seems like they want to do a story about Peggy's rescue."

Kerry shrugged. "That's all right with me. There's been so many townspeople who've expressed their interest and concern in my daughter. It would give me a chance to let them know how grateful I am." She settled her gaze on his face. "To them and to you."

Being grateful to him wasn't exactly what Jared wanted from Kerry, but if it would help to give him a chance to get to know her better, he'd have to play upon it. At least, for the time being.

"I'm glad you feel that way," he said, "because I told the reporter the three of us would meet him tomorrow evening at my house."

Kerry's brows slowly lifted as she took in the full meaning of his words. "You told him that without asking me first?"

The incredulous tone in her voice said she wasn't happy and it dawned on Jared that this woman was unlike any he'd pursued in the past. He'd never had to work at getting a woman's attention, much less in making her like him. With Kerry it seemed like everything he did was wrong.

"Uh—yes, I did. I didn't think you'd want to refuse the newspaper. Especially when the whole area is interested in reading about Peggy's rescue."

Her soft lips compressed together and Jared wondered how it would feel to take her in his arms and coax her lips apart with a kiss.

"Giving the story to the newspaper has nothing to do with it," she clipped. "We could have met him at the library, a restaurant, anywhere but your home!"

Jared looked truly offended. "And what's the matter with my house? You probably don't even know where I live."

She heaved out a breath as she focused her gaze on Peggy. At the moment, the two animals were stretched out on the grass near Peggy as she tempted both cat and dog to catch the dandelion in her hand. Her daughter was safe and healthy because this man had risked his life, Kerry thought. And now she was playing and giggling because this man had brought her a special gift. She couldn't be annoyed with him. Even if she tried.

"I didn't even know you lived around Black Arrow," she admitted.

"Well, I only live here when I'm not away on a job," he conceded. "But I keep a place south of town. The old Wafford farm. Know where that is?"

Kerry nodded, surprised to hear he chose to keep residence in an old farmhouse rather than an easy-living apartment in town. "I rarely have any reason to go out that way. I thought the house was empty."

He grinned. "Oh, I show my face around here every so often. If I didn't my brothers and sisters would disown me."

The idea that he was only here in Black Arrow temporarily was enough to allow Kerry to relax her guard. The man would be gone soon, she reasoned with herself. He wasn't trying to get involved with her. And she knew not to let herself get interested in him. There wouldn't be time enough or a reason for anything heartbreaking to happen.

"Okay, Peggy and I will be there," she told him. "What time?"

"The reporter will be there at seven. Make it a few minutes before so I'll have time to show you around the old place."

She turned her head toward him and as soon as their eyes met, her heart leaped with forbidden excitement. "We'll be there at a quarter till," she promised.

"Kerry, I don't want you to do this. Call the man right now and tell him you're not coming."

Kerry continued to study her image in the mirror rather than look at her mother who'd entered the bedroom moments ago. "Don't do this to me, Mom. Not now."

Shaking her head, Enola sank onto the foot of Kerry's bed. "You're making a big mistake."

Kerry sighed. Ever since her mother had learned about the interview at Jared's house tonight, she'd been treating Kerry as though she were sixteen years old rather than twenty-six. "I'm going to do an interview for the newspaper, Mom. This isn't some life-or-death mission."

Enola clamped her jaws together. "It isn't like you to be disrespectful, Kerry. Is that what this man is doing to you?"

Kerry adjusted the soft beige blouse she'd tucked into a broomstick skirt which was printed in narrow stripes of black, beige and turquoise. The clothes were feminine, she decided, but casual enough so as not to appear she'd gone to pains to dress up for him.

"Jared Colton hasn't done anything to me. Except save my daughter's life."

Enola tossed her hands into the air. "He wasn't the

only man there that night. The firemen, the lawmen, the emergency people were all working to get Peggy out.''

"That's right. And I'll always be grateful to them,'' Kerry agreed, determined not to let her mother's comments rile her.

"Jared Colton isn't a hero.''

"I didn't say he was. Neither has he.'' She glanced over her shoulder toward the door. "Is Peggy still watching television? I don't want her to get her dress dirty.''

Impatient with her daughter's effort to change the subject, Enola said, "She's watching Mr. Rogers and the doors are locked so she can't go outside.''

"Good. We need to leave in five minutes.''

Enola rose from the bed and joined Kerry at the dresser mirror. "Kerry, I'm trying to talk to you about this for your own good. You may think Jared Colton's harmless, but let's face it, you're not a good judge of character when it comes to men.''

With slow deliberation, Kerry picked up a hairbrush and began to pull it through her thick hair. "What is that supposed to mean, Mom?''

Enola reached out and gripped her daughter's shoulder. "You thought Damon was a wonderful man. You thought he would give you a nice home with children. Instead, he was using you. If you'd used better judgment, Peggy might've had a father that wanted her.''

Not at any time since Kerry had returned from Virginia, pregnant and heartbroken, had her mother said such hurtful things to her. To learn that Enola thought in these terms filled her with sadness and a firm resolution to start looking for a home of her own. Something she should have done right after Peggy was born.

"Yes, I suppose you're right. I messed up. I let myself behave like a normal woman."

"Kerry—"

"Sorry, Mom. I've got to go."

Before Enola could say more, Kerry grabbed up her handbag and hurried out to fetch Peggy from in front of the television.

"You won't be late, will you?" Enola asked as she watched her daughter and grandchild head out the door.

"I don't know. But don't worry. I'll have my cell phone with me in case I have car trouble," Kerry told her. Even though she knew that car trouble was the last thing Enola would be worried about.

When Jared spotted Kerry's compact car heading up the drive, he trotted off the porch and met her at the yard fence.

Immediately Peggy reached for him and he made a big display of tossing her up in the crook of his arm and raving over her pretty pink dress.

"Did you wear that just for me, little dove?"

She nodded. "Mama says I look pretty in it."

He chuckled. "And your mama is right. You look as pretty as she does."

Jared's eyes slanted toward Kerry and she could feel a warm blush slide up her neck and onto her cheeks. She couldn't remember the last time a man had told her she was pretty. Clarence sometimes remarked on her hair or her clothing, but their relationship was a father-daughter thing. Hearing such a compliment from a man like Jared was something altogether different.

"Good evening, Jared. Are we late? I accidentally ran by the turnoff to your house."

He gestured for her to precede him through the yard

gate. As Kerry stepped into the yard, she noticed he was dressed a bit more formal this evening. Instead of the jeans and pullovers she'd seen him in the past few days, he was wearing khaki chinos and a pale yellow button-down shirt with long sleeves. Brown roper boots were on his feet and a brown leather belt studded with small chunks of turquoise circled his trim waist.

"You're just right," he assured her. "Would you like to go in and have something to drink or would you rather look around the place first?"

Kerry stepped inside the yard. "Let's look around," she said.

Nodding in agreement, he placed Peggy back on the ground and quickly reached for the child's hand. "Okay, let's walk around the house and then I'll show you the inside and how a messy bachelor lives," he added with a devilish wink, then settled his free hand against Kerry's back as though touching her was a natural thing.

The contact was electric, sending ripples of heat radiating out from his fingers. Instantly, her mind shouted at her to move away and keep a formal distance from him. Yet his closeness made her feel feminine and special. Something she'd not felt in a long time.

As the three of them strolled beneath large shade trees, Jared explained to Kerry how the Wafford farm had once produced maize, but since the land had sold, the ground had turned fallow.

When Kerry noticed the fittings of a natural gas pipeline jutting up from the ground not more than fifty yards away from the back of the house, she asked, "Did a gas company hit gas on your land?"

Jared chuckled. "I'm not that lucky. I only rent this place. And I don't think Mr. Wafford owned the mineral rights, so he didn't get anything out of it, either. Except surface damages to his field. I think that's part of the reason he decided to move into town and forget about farming.''

As they walked around the back yard, Peggy spotted a swing suspended from a limb of a huge sycamore tree. The little girl raced over and jumped into the board seat fastened to two thickly braided grass ropes. Jared followed and gave her a few pushes to put the swing in motion.

Peggy's squeals of delight were like music to Kerry's ears. To see her daughter so happy and relaxed was enough to tell Kerry she'd made the right decision to come out here tonight.

''This is a pretty place,'' Kerry told him. ''But I'm very surprised that you live here.''

His black brows piqued with interest as he glanced at her. ''Why? Even men like me need a place to hang their hat once in a while.''

''A man like you?'' she asked, wondering if he was referring to his job or his rambling ways with women.

''I'm a petroleum engineer,'' he explained. ''I never know where my job will take me.''

He lifted Peggy from the swing. ''Come on, little dove, we'd better go in the house and get ready for our company.''

Moments later, Jared ushered them into the living room by way of the front door. Kerry was immediately surprised by the neat hominess that met her curious gaze. Most of the stuffed furniture dated back to the 1940s. Braided rugs were scattered here and there across the faded flowers on the linoleum floor, with the largest one lying in front of a native rock fireplace.

In contrast to the older furniture, an entertainment

center took up a small wall opposite the couch. Pictures of people she recognized as his family were displayed throughout the room on end tables, wall shelves and the fireplace mantle.

Nothing about the room was what Kerry had been expecting. Maybe because she'd always considered Jared Colton a smooth operator. A man that most likely lived in an impersonal apartment where the only thing he needed was a change of clothes and enough space to entertain a lady friend. Now she could see she'd been wrong in stereotyping him in such a way.

While her thoughts and her gaze had been rambling, Jared had led Peggy over to a small school desk in one corner of the room.

Kerry now watched her daughter wiggle eagerly on the seat as Jared placed a magazine full of wildlife in front of her.

"She likes animals," Jared said as he returned to Kerry's side. "That ought to keep her busy for a few minutes."

Kerry found it was impossible not to smile at him. "Where did you learn about entertaining children?"

Jared chuckled. "I don't know anything about children," he confessed. "I've just been playing it all by ear."

"Well, Peggy seems to think you do everything right," she told him.

But did Peggy's mother, Jared wondered. Up until now he'd never met a woman he couldn't read. Even her smiles were enigmatic. And the mystery of not knowing exactly what was going on in her head made her even more attractive to Jared.

"How has Peggy been doing today? Does she still like her new kitten?" he asked.

The image of Peggy pushing Claws around in her baby buggy put a soft smile on Kerry's lips. "They're inseparable. I think Fred is starting to get jealous."

Jared chuckled as his gaze slid slowly, seductively over her face. "I don't blame him. We males don't like another male horning in on our territory."

The possessive gleam in his gray eyes reminded her of a determined wolf, resolute in catching his prey. Slivers of anticipation rippled down her spine and warned her this man was too dangerous to play with.

Pregnant moments began to pass as they stared at one another. Kerry figured if the room had been dark, anyone could have seen the flashes of fire arcing between their bodies. In all of her life she'd never felt so spellbound.

"And just where is your territory?" she finally asked.

One corner of his mouth lifted in a sensual grin. "I haven't marked it. Yet."

Kerry was struggling to think of something to say to that, when a knock on the door saved her.

As Jared went to usher the newspaper reporter into the house, she told herself this was the last time she could allow herself to be in Jared Colton's company. He was simply too masculine, too downright dangerous for a woman who'd already suffered a broken heart.

Chapter Four

The reporter was a rail-thin man somewhere in his mid-fifties with graying hair and an affable smile. After he'd introduced himself as Luther and explained to Kerry and Jared just exactly what he wanted, he proceeded to pose the three of them for a photograph.

Before Kerry knew it, she found herself wedged next to Jared on a small couch while her daughter was artfully positioned on her rescuer's lap. All the while the reporter snapped his camera, Kerry kept thinking the whole thing was more like an intimate family portrait than a news story photo. Husband and wife cuddled on a loveseat with their small daughter on her daddy's lap. She could only imagine what her mother and friends were going to think when they saw it in the newspaper.

To make matters worse, once the picture-taking ended, Kerry had every intention of rising and finding another seat in the room. But before she could make her escape, Luther pulled a nearby wooden rocker right in front of them for his own seat and began to fire questions. Kerry had no choice but to remain on the couch with her shoulder and thigh jammed against Jared.

Forty-five long minutes later, Luther finally packed up his camera and notebook and left with the promise that they'd see the article in tomorrow's edition of the *Black Arrow Times*. By then Kerry didn't care if she ever saw the piece. Being so close to Jared had left her as jumpy as a cat. Especially when he'd spent the bigger part of the interview grinning at her.

"Well, that wasn't so bad," Jared said cheerfully after he'd shut the door behind the departing Luther. "I'll bet he'll only get half the story twisted."

"Twisted?" Kerry asked in surprise. "Why should he do that? We told him exactly how everything happened."

Jared chuckled as he walked back to where Kerry was still sitting on the couch. "Yeah, but it always somehow gets changed when it's transcribed to paper. Just ask Bram. I doubt there's been one time since he's become the county sheriff that he's been quoted correctly."

Kerry quickly rose to her feet. "Well, I don't suppose it matters all that much. As long as the readers understand that you got Peggy out of that horrible hole without hurting her."

All during the interview, Kerry had stressed several times to the reporter that if it hadn't been for Jared, Peggy might still be trapped beneath the ground. Her words of praise had touched him then. And they did so even more now that the two of them were alone. "You're giving me too much credit, Kerry."

She gave him a brief smile. "I don't think so," she said, then glanced over at Peggy who was lying on the floor quietly watching cartoons that Jared had turned on to keep the child occupied during the long interview. From the looks of her drowsy expression, Kerry knew her daughter would be asleep in just a few minutes.

"Well, I'd better head toward home," she told Jared. "Peggy needs to get to bed soon."

Frowning, Jared glanced at his watch. "It's not that late. It's only just now gotten dark. Why don't you stay long enough to have some coffee and cookies before you go. They're homemade," he added temptingly.

She breathed deeply as the urge to stay warred with her common sense. For the past three and a half years Kerry had deliberately shied away from any sort of personal contact with men. And for the most part, she'd been content. She'd not seen any reason to risk putting herself through that sort of hell again. But being with Jared reminded her of just how much she was missing in life.

"Homemade cookies," she said with a wry smile. "Don't tell me you baked them."

He laughed. "No. I'm a fry cook, but other than that forget it. My sister was sweet enough to bring these over yesterday. So I saved them for this evening."

Kerry cast another thoughtful glance at her daughter. Peggy's eyes were already drooping. Even if she left right now, the child would be asleep before they reached the main highway. It wouldn't make much difference to let her sleep here at Jared's.

"All right," she agreed. "But let me put Peggy on the couch first. She's almost asleep."

She started after her daughter, but Jared quickly caught her by the arm. "No. I'll get her."

Kerry stood back and allowed him to pick Peggy up from the floor and gently carry her limp little body to the couch. After he'd carefully tucked a throw pillow beneath her head, he glanced at Kerry. "Is she okay like this? Or does she need to be covered with something?"

Even though the house was air-conditioned, it was not cool enough to make Peggy chilled. "She's fine," Kerry told him. "Thank you."

Jared started to move away from the couch, then paused to reach down and smooth a wayward black curl away from Peggy's cheek. "She's quite an angel," he said with a sheepish smile.

"Angels don't crawl into dirty drainpipes," Kerry reminded him.

Laughing softly, he moved away from the couch and with his hand at Kerry's back guided her toward the kitchen. "Well, even an angel can be momentarily distracted."

Like the living area, the kitchen was equipped with older type appliances and fixtures, but everything appeared clean and efficient. At one end of the long room, a rattan-shaded lamp swung over a pine farm table covered with a yellow-and-white plaid tablecloth. In the middle sat a mason jar filled with wildflowers of all colors and sizes.

The feminine touch of his sister, no doubt, Kerry thought. Jared was the hard hat, work boots sort. She doubted he'd ever picked a wildflower in his life. Except maybe the kind with two legs and painted lips.

"Have a seat," he invited, "and I'll make some coffee. It's a quick drip pot so it won't take but a couple of minutes.''

While he gathered the coffee makings at the cabinet counter, Kerry took a seat at the end of the farm table. To her left, a double window was covered with green-and-yellow tiers that matched the table cloth. Another sign that a woman had done some decorating in the house.

Across the room, Jared spoke up. ''I hope your mother didn't give you a bad time about coming over here this evening.''

Kerry wasn't about to tell him exactly what her mother had said. It was too humiliating. ''I'm a grown woman, but she still wants to treat me as if I'm a teenager,'' Kerry told him.

He carried a plate of chocolate chip and pecan cookies over to the table and placed it in front of her. ''Some parents are like that,'' he empathized, then added in a nostalgic voice, ''I sometimes wonder what my mom would be saying to me if she was alive today. Probably that I'm getting old and I need to find a nice girl and settle down.''

The wry grin that followed his words said he considered the idea amusing. Apparently he'd never had a hankering for one special woman and a few little Coltons to call his own, Kerry decided.

Beneath the soft glow of the lamp, Kerry's eyes searched his strong profile. ''You hardly look old,'' she pointed out.

''Thirty-four. That may not sound old, but my father was married and had several children by the time he was my age.''

''Your parents were killed in a plane crash, weren't they?''

He nodded with a sad sort of acceptance. "In 1987. They were vacationing in New Mexico and their small plane was caught in an unexpected blizzard. It went down south of Taos."

Kerry sipped the coffee, then said, "I didn't really know Sally or Trevor, but I remember when the accident happened. I must have been about eleven at the time and I kept thinking how awful it would be not to have my mother and father."

Jared sighed. "It was awful, Kerry. For all five of us. Especially my younger sister Willow. She was only sixteen at the time. But I think having siblings to lean on always makes hard times a little easier to bear. And it helped that our grandmother, Gloria, was around to fill in a part of the gap."

"Is she still living?" Kerry asked curiously.

Jared nodded. "Gran lives with Willow over the feed store. And her father, George, is still living, too."

The cookie in Kerry's hand paused in midair. "You have a great-grandfather?"

A smile of genuine fondness spread across Jared's face. "Oh yes. Great-grandfather lives in the country about thirty minutes or so from Black Arrow. In the same house he's always lived in. We grandchildren have tried to talk him into selling the place and moving into town, but he won't hear of it. That's always been his home and he wouldn't give up his livestock for anything. Thankfully he has one neighbor that keeps a pretty close eye on him."

Kerry shook her head with amazement. Other than Enola, she had a maternal grandmother who lived about fifty miles north in Anadarko. What little was left of her father's people were scattered in some of the western states. Since they were never interested in her father

Marvin's family while he'd been alive, she hardly expected to hear from them in the future.

"It must be wonderful to have a relative who has lived that long and seen so many changes in our world. I'm sure he has many stories to tell."

Laughter rolled from Jared's mouth and as Kerry's gaze drank in his bronze features, she could see why women had always been drawn to him. His happy, laid-back manner coupled with his rough-hewn looks made him a heady force to reckon with.

"Stories! Grandfather George is so full of tales we're not sure where the real ones end and the fiction begins. He's one of the few pure Comanches still living around here and he doesn't let any of his family forget it. Our heritage is important to him."

Kerry's expression brightened. "I think that's wonderful," she said, then just as suddenly a wistfulness came over her. "My father didn't know much at all about his heritage. And he didn't care enough to learn."

"What about Enola? She's Comanche, too, isn't she?"

Kerry nodded. "Enola is proud of the fact that she's Native American but that's about as far as it goes. I guess she's always been too busy just trying to survive to think about much else. But I've been trying to teach Peggy about our ancestors as much as I can. Of course, she's too young to understand much yet. But I think it's important to start with her early so that she'll get a sense of being a Comanche as she grows up."

"Then you should let me take the two of you to see George sometime. He loves company. But be warned he's hard to get away from and before you leave you'll probably hear about a vision."

Kerry smiled with fascination. "A vision? Does he really have visions?"

Jared chuckled. "Who knows. None of us actually believe he has that ability. But the crazy thing about it is that most of what he tells us winds up coming true."

Just hearing about his grandfather made Kerry's brown eyes glow. "I don't know if you realize it, Jared, but you're a very lucky man."

His grin was wicked. "Why? Because I'm sitting here eating cookies with you?"

She glanced away from him as another blush warmed her face. Did he really find her company that pleasant? she wondered. It was hard to imagine. She didn't have to look in the mirror to know she was about as glamorous and exciting as Betty Crocker. And no one had to tell her that Jared Colton's taste in women ran toward the beautiful and vivacious.

During her waitressing days at Woody's, it wasn't uncommon to see him with a different belle every night. He'd had his pick of the most attractive girls to be had in Black Arrow and she seriously doubted that had changed. Especially now that he was in the prime of good looks, along with being a successful engineer. There was no reason why he'd settle for someone like Kerry.

She breathed deeply and told herself to ignore the glint in his eyes and forget the notion that she was sitting here alone with a man who made women his number one pastime.

"You're lucky because you have so much family," she finally managed to say. "Close family."

Her looked at her with faint surprise. "I guess I never thought of us Coltons as lucky. Especially with our parents getting killed. But you're right. I can't imagine what life would be like without my brothers and sisters. And we also have six cousins and their parents, Aunt Alice and Uncle Thomas, who was my dad's twin. If any family member has trouble, the rest are always ready to gather around and help.''

Kerry nodded. ''I noticed some of your relatives were there to help that night you were trying to rescue Peggy from the pipe.''

''Yeah, I guess they were,'' he said while thinking Enola had been the only relative there to support Kerry through the awful incident. It was no wonder she considered his large family a blessing. There had to be times that she felt very alone. ''And I guess I'm guilty of taking my big family for granted. Maybe I should thank Willow again for making these cookies,'' he added with a chuckle.

Kerry smiled in agreement. ''Yes, I think you should. They're very good.''

He nudged the plate toward her. ''Then have another. You've only eaten one.''

''Oh no. One's enough.'' She glanced at her half-empty mug. ''I really should finish my coffee and go. It'll be late by the time I drive home.'' And Enola would be champing at the bit, she thought wearily.

Disappointment struck him as he realized he didn't want her to leave. She had a quiet, sweet nature that invited him to relax, to talk about things he rarely thought about, much less discussed over a cup of coffee. Talk. The word put an inward smile on his face. Since when had talking to a woman been important? he asked himself.

''We haven't been sitting here long, Kerry. Finish your coffee and tell me about yourself—what you do.''

Her brows lifted in surprise. ''What I do?''

"Sure. I know you can't still work at Woody's 'cause that place was turned into a dry cleaners a few years ago."

The idea that he still remembered her after all this time was wildly flattering. Which only proved that her mother was right about one thing, she was a fool when it came to men.

"I work at Liberty National Bank. In the note department."

Since Jared didn't use that particular bank, the chances of his seeing Kerry around town before the incident with Peggy would have been slim. Especially when he figured she didn't do much socializing.

"Do you like your job or is it just a stepping stone to what you'd really like to do?"

Since Peggy had been born, no one had bothered to ask Kerry that question. Not even her own mother. Enola's attitude was that Kerry should be grateful to have any sort of job in order to support her young daughter. The idea that Jared cared enough to ask made her feel special, something she'd not felt in a long time.

"I like the job. Everyone there is easy to work with and the pay is okay. But it's not what I want to do for the rest of my life."

When she didn't elaborate, he leaned back in his chair and folded his arms across his chest. "I feel like a dentist trying to pull a tooth with the patient's mouth clamped shut," he joked, then made a rolling motion with one hand. "Come on, what is the thing you'd want to be doing if you could?"

Her finger slowly traced the plaid pattern in the tablecloth as she thought about all the hopes and dreams she'd pushed aside in order to raise her daughter. Some people might view the choices she'd made as sacrifices. But Kerry didn't see them that way. Peggy was worth much, much more than anything she'd had to give up.

"I need a few more hours to acquire my master's degree in business. Someday when that happens I'd like to get a job with a small investment firm and work my way up to a high-level position." She cast him a rueful smile. "But that will be in the far future—when Peggy is much older."

Jared didn't have to ask what had delayed her education. She'd had a baby. And she'd gone straight to work to support her. He desperately wanted to ask her about the father and why they weren't together now. But he instinctively knew that Kerry didn't feel comfortable enough to tell him something that personal. More than likely she'd be offended if he asked. But he was going to get closer to her, he promised himself. And soon.

Anxious now to break the cozy atmosphere that seemed to be curling around them and drawing them together, Kerry quickly rose from her seat. "I really should be going. It would be embarrassing if Mom called your brother Bram out to search for me."

Rising to his feet, he grinned at her. "Why Kerry, I didn't realize you could actually joke."

She tried to prevent her lips from tilting upward, but a smile spread across her face anyway. "I can laugh, too. Sometimes," she tossed back at him as she headed out of the kitchen.

Jared followed close on her heels and appreciated the chance to watch the gentle sway of her hips as she walked. The faint sultry scent of her perfume drifted back to him like the luring curl of a finger. Her body would be soft, he thought. Soft and warm and womanly and the urge to reach out and touch her was so strong he jammed his hands into his trouser pockets.

When they reached the living room, Jared said, "I'll carry Peggy out to the car for you."

Kerry grabbed her handbag and preceded him out to the car where he placed the sleeping child on the back seat.

"We need to buckle her up somehow," he said in a hushed voice so as not to wake her. "I didn't save this little darlin' from a dark hole to have her hurt in a car accident."

As Kerry watched his fingers smooth Peggy's long hair and ruffled dress, her heart turned as soft as warm butter. Jared might not know what it was like to have a child of his own, yet he treated Peggy with as much love and tenderness as any father would.

All at once Kerry realized her head was hovering very near to Jared's. With the slightest turn, their faces would be together, their lips separated by only a scant distance. Just the thought of kissing Jared Colton sent a thrill of heat rushing from her head to her toes.

The decadent thoughts turned her voice to a throaty whisper. "I've buckled her up like this before. And I'll drive slowly on the way home."

Thankfully he eased back out of the car and Kerry was able to breathe normally again, but her nervous hands fumbled with the seat belt straps before she was finally able to get them completely fastened.

Once she had Peggy safely settled, Kerry hurried around to the driver's side of the car. Jared followed and opened the door before she could do it herself.

"This has been nice, Kerry. I'm glad you agreed to come out tonight."

His low, masculine voice was as smooth as the warm

night breeze slipping over her bare skin. Her heart thudding, Kerry tucked her hair behind her ears and glanced his way. "Thank you, Jared. It has been nice."

Before he could stop himself, Jared stepped closer and gently folded his fingers around her upper arm. "Uh—when are we going to get together again?"

Eyes wide, she stared up at him. Maybe in the back of her mind, she'd suspected he was slightly attracted to her. But she'd assured herself he would never act upon his attraction. Not when he could find more beautiful, willing women elsewhere.

"I—don't think that would be a good idea," she finally managed to murmur.

A scowl pulled his black brows together. "Why not? Is there someone you're seeing on a regular basis?"

Kerry had lived such an isolated life since her ordeal with Damon that his question seemed ludicrous. Averting her gaze from his, she released a shaky laugh. "No."

Jared continued to frown as he studied her lowered head. "Is there something funny about that question?"

Kerry lifted her eyes back to his and suddenly she felt overwhelmed with emptiness. Damon had not only shattered her hopes and dreams of having a family, he'd also filled her with a deep distrust of men. In the past three, nearly four years, she'd not met one man she'd felt comfortable enough to share a hamburger with, much less date on a continued basis. Yet as she looked at Jared, she desperately wished that things could be different.

"Not exactly," she answered, then tried her best to smile. The last thing she wanted Jared Colton to think was that she was limping around with hidden scars. "I just—don't date."

Jared had suspected she didn't have much of a social life. At least not with the opposite sex. But to hear her say she didn't date at all was a real tragedy.

"Oh come on, Kerry, you're kidding, aren't you?"

Her lips thinned to a grim line. "No. I'm not kidding."

He looked totally perplexed. "But why?"

Why? Was he blind, she wondered. Wasn't Peggy's existence enough explanation for him? "That's something I don't want to get into." Especially with you, she silently added.

Jared could see her expression closing him off, and the separation left him with a sudden emptiness. "Okay," he said with slow deliberation. "You don't have to get into your reasons right now. But I might as well warn you that I won't take no for an answer."

His remark made Kerry even more aware of his warm fingers pressing into her flesh. For one reckless moment, she considered tossing her fears aside and simply stepping into his arms. Somehow she knew that to kiss this man would be a wild, sweet pleasure. To make love to him would bend her mind and make her forget everything. Until it was over and he was gone.

That cool thought of sanity was the only thing that gave her the strength to pull away from him and slip into the driver's seat.

With her hands gripping the wheel, she said, "And I might as well warn you that you're wasting your time. I have a child and a job that requires all my focus. I don't have any space in my life for men."

To Kerry's surprise he gave her a broad grin.

"That's good to hear, 'cause I only want you to make room for one man. Me."

Kerry wasn't prepared to deal with this sudden intimate exchange. She'd expected after tonight their time together would end once and for all. And it had to, she thought desperately. Jared Colton was the last man who could fit into her life.

Her hands shaking, she shut the door and quickly started the engine. "Goodbye, Jared."

He reached through the window and laid a hand on her shoulder. "You'd better buckle up before you drive away," he said dryly.

Flustered from his touch and the fact that she was letting him get to her, she snatched up the belt and fumbled with the two ends until they snapped together.

"That's better," he said smugly. Then pulling his hand from her shoulder, he tapped the door in a gesture of farewell. "See you later, Kerry."

Even though she'd already pulled the gearshift into Reverse, she pressed on the brake and looked through the window at him. "Jared, I expect you to respect my wishes."

His brows lifted with flirty innocence and he bent his head toward the open window. "And what are your wishes?" he asked softly.

Kerry silently groaned. No man should be allowed to be this sexy or tempting, she thought desperately. It wasn't fair to womankind. "That you not try to see me again. For any reason."

A twisted grin lifted one corner of his mouth. "We both know you don't really wish that, Kerry."

Kerry was all set to argue, but Jared didn't give her the chance. Before she could make any sort of response, he waved goodbye and stepped back from the car.

Grateful for the chance to escape, she stepped on the

gas and wheeled the car around. As she drove away, her eyes longed to find him in the rearview mirror. But she refused to look up or to acknowledge that Jared Colton had left her shaking from her head to her toes.

Chapter Five

The newspaper landed with a plop on the keyboard of Kerry's computer. Frowning at the interruption, she looked up from the screen to see Christa's grinning face.

"What's up?" Kerry asked. "Have you already run out of something to do?"

Giggling, Christa glanced over her shoulder to make sure none of the bosses were nearby. "Actually my desk is loaded with work, but I just had to see if you'd had a chance to look at the paper yet."

Her face blank, Kerry shook her head. "The paper?"

"Kerry!" Christa practically shouted. "Have you forgotten? You and the town's new hero!"

Dear Lord, since she'd left Jared's house last night all she'd been able to think about was him. The newspaper article had totally slipped her mind.

Snatching up the paper she began to flip through the pages.

"Try the front page," Christa said smugly. "Lower left-hand corner. It's hard to miss."

Kerry flopped the paper back over then gasped as her gaze zeroed in on the photo. Just as she'd feared last night, the image was more like a snapshot at a family reunion.

"Oh, this is—" she paused and miserably shook her head. "What was that reporter thinking? The three of us look like we're posed for a family Christmas card!"

"You do look right at home with each other," Christa said with another giggle. "So tell me, what was it like being that close to Jared Colton?"

Kerry glowered at the other woman. "What sort of question is that?"

Christa tossed another covert glance behind her just to make sure the two of them weren't being observed. "Oh come on, Kerry. I know you don't go out on dates. But that doesn't mean you're totally dead. Jared Colton is a real hunk. Surely your heart was doing some sort of tap dance while the two of you were rubbing shoulders."

Her heart had been dancing all right, Kerry silently admitted. But she'd done her best to ignore the affliction. And she was going to keep right on ignoring the strange feelings she got every time she thought about the man.

"He is a handsome man, Christa," Kerry said firmly. "But that doesn't mean anything to me."

Christa leaned over the front of the desk and picked up Kerry's wrist. "Better let me take your pulse, lady. You're definitely not normal."

Kerry shook her hand away from Christa's fingers,

then shoved the newspaper under a stack of banking forms. "Look Christa, the reason you don't think I'm normal is because my common sense is much stronger than my libido."

The blonde slapped a hand across her forehead and lifted her eyes toward the ceiling. "Okay, I admit my marriage was a disaster and, like you, I picked a guy that couldn't have been worse for me. But that doesn't mean I've stopped being a woman. And—" she lowered her head and leveled a pointed look on Kerry "—you haven't stopped being one either."

Kerry knew if she protested too loudly here it would only make Christa suspicious and the last thing she wanted was for anyone to think there was something going on between her and Jared.

Sighing, she said, "All right. I admit I still think about men. I even wish I could find a perfect father for Peggy. But that doesn't mean I let a handsome face and sexy body turn my head. Most anyone in this town would agree that Jared Colton is a confirmed bachelor. He's not the sort of man a serious woman would look at twice. Unless she wanted her heart broken."

"Hmm. You could be right. But he looked right at home in that picture."

Kerry laughed. "That's because he was home, Christa. Now get out of here and let me get back to work. I promised Clarence to have these papers finished before noon and at this rate it will be noon tomorrow."

Christa made a tsking noise of disapproval as she started toward the door. "All work and no play. When do you ever have any fun, Kerry?"

Kerry was still thinking about that question long after Christa had disappeared from sight.

* * *

When Kerry arrived home that evening after work, two neighbors were on the front porch with Enola. The sight of the women made Kerry groan with dread. She'd already spent most of the day discussing the newspaper article. Now that she was home, she didn't want to have to go over it again. But both women appeared to be comfortably glued to their lawn chairs as they waited for her to climb out of the car.

"Kerry! We're so glad you got home before we left. We want to know what it's like to be a town celebrity."

The remark came from Helen, a large, gray-haired woman who'd raised three sons close to Kerry's age.

"I'm not really a celebrity, Helen," she said with a weary smile. "The only reason my picture is in the paper is because I'm Peggy's mother."

Alice, a small woman with dark hair, quickly spoke up, "Oh, you're being modest, honey. All three of you are celebrities now. Everyone in Black Arrow is talking about this." She tapped a red fingernail against the paper in her lap.

"That's right," Helen put in. "Just about everyone is saying what a lucky thing that Jared Colton was back in town when Peggy got trapped. That young man is a real hero. If it hadn't been for him—well, I'd hate to think what would have happened to little Peggy."

"And it sure doesn't hurt that he's as cute as a bug in a rug," Alice added with a wink. "I wouldn't mind getting my picture taken with him. Not at all."

"Do you know if he's back in town to stay?" Helen asked.

Did these women really think she would know something that personal about Jared Colton? Kerry wondered. Just because he'd plucked her daughter from the jaws of the earth, didn't mean there was any sort of intimacy between them.

"I wouldn't know," Kerry said dully. "But I seriously doubt it. Jared follows his job."

Alice sighed as though she was thirty years younger and still in the market for a man. "Well, the way he has his arm around you in this picture, I'd say he'd rather be following you."

A few feet away in another lawn chair, Enola cleared her throat. "Kerry, you'd probably better go check on Peggy. It's about time she woke from her nap."

Kerry knew exactly why her mother was interrupting. Just the thought of anyone linking her daughter to Jared in a romantic way was enough to send Enola into spasms. And normally Kerry would have resented her interference. But not this time. Thoughts of Jared had tormented her all day. She needed an escape.

"Sure, Mom," Kerry said, then quickly excused herself to the two women.

Inside the house, she went straight to the bedroom she shared with her daughter. Peggy was still asleep, her face buried in the faded patchwork quilt covering the bed. Not wanting to disturb her, Kerry quietly changed from her office clothes into shorts and a T-shirt, then slipped out of the room.

She was in the kitchen, making herself a glass of iced tea when the telephone rang. For a moment, she considered not answering. She'd heard all she wanted to hear about Jared Colton's heroism. Yet she knew if she ignored the ringing, Enola would hear it and come to answer the phone herself.

With a weary sigh, Kerry carried her glass over to the wall phone which was situated at one end of the cabinets.

"Hello."

"Kerry, it's Jared."

The deep voice momentarily stunned her. He was the last person she'd expected to be hearing from today. Especially after she'd made an issue of not wanting to see him again.

"Jared—why are you calling?"

"I wanted to see what you thought about our article."

She didn't bother to stifle her groan. "Not you, too."

Jared chuckled. "I take it you've been getting a lot of response over it."

"I could hardly work with all the people stopping by my office and calling on the telephone. There's two neighbors out on the porch right now who are probably still singing your praises to Mom."

He chuckled again. "Oh, I don't expect that's going over too well."

"No. But they're old friends. After a while she'll tell them to shut up. Especially Alice. She thinks you're as cute as a bug in a rug."

"I'm not really worried about what Alice thinks. I'd like to know what Kerry thinks."

One hand gripped the receiver while the other tightened its hold on the icy glass of tea. "I think I should have never agreed to that interview last night. Now people are starting to think that we—well, I'm not sure all of them are reading the article. I think most of them are just looking at the three of us hugged up together like mama bear, daddy bear and baby bear."

Jared's loud laughter sounded in her ear. "Kerry, I really don't know how you can be so funny when every bone in your body is the serious kind."

She swallowed down a few sips of tea in an effort

to loosen the ball of nerves in her throat. "Look, Jared, I told you last night—"

"Please don't go into that again. I remember everything you told me. And I have no intentions of letting that stop me from trying to see you again. So what about having dinner with me? Tonight?"

Jared Colton was asking her out on a bona fide date. Kerry couldn't deny that she was thrilled he found her attractive. After all, there wasn't a woman on earth who didn't want to be desired by a man. Yet the part of her that Damon had crushed was very afraid.

She breathed in a deep bracing breath. "Don't you ever work?"

Once again his soft laughter met her ear. The sound was so seductive, it was all she could do to keep from shivering.

"I'm working now, Kerry. If you walked out to the open field behind your house and looked toward the site, you could see me standing beside my pickup truck."

"Well, then keep working and forget about having dinner with me," she said as sternly as she could.

"I have to eat and so do you."

"I already had Peggy out late last night. I'm not about to take her out two nights in a row."

"I wasn't planning on taking Peggy with us."

Even though she wasn't looking at him, she could easily envision his gray eyes glinting sexily back at her.

"You're crazy if you think I'd go without Peggy."

"That's easy to fix. We'll take Peggy with us."

She rolled her eyes. "No. We have nothing in common, Jared. And you've already said yourself that you'll be leaving once your job is finished."

His sigh was full of frustration. "Kerry, this isn't a

marriage proposal. I'm just asking you to have a meal with me. As two friends. Nothing more.''

''Why would you want to do that?'' she asked suspiciously.

There was a long pause, then he said, ''I'm not sure what that question means.''

Expecting her mother to walk into the room at any moment, Kerry moved as far as the coiled cord would allow in order to peer through the straight shot of rooms to the front of the house. Through the open screen door, she could see Alice's crossed legs. Apparently the two neighbors were keeping Enola occupied.

In a hushed voice, she said, ''Jared, I'm not stupid. You don't need to bother yourself with me just to have female company.''

He clicked his tongue with disapproval. ''Kerry, you don't believe all those old rumors you've heard about me, do you?''

''Yes.''

He laughed. ''Then you have to give me a chance to plead my case. And Kerry, just so you understand, I want your company. Not just female company.''

How could she resist him when the hungry, lonely part of her heart was begging her to reach out to him.

''Like I said, I won't take Peggy out again tonight.''

''Then tomorrow night?''

Her heart began to hammer at what she was about to do. ''All right. Tomorrow night.''

''Good. I'll pick you up at six-thirty,'' he said with undisguised pleasure. ''And Kerry, it doesn't matter what you wear, just so you're wearing a smile.''

''Goodbye, Jared. I'll see you tomorrow evening.''

* * *

Early the next morning, Jared was using a laser instrument to shoot the correct angle of the new pipeline his crew was laying when he heard one of the workmen yell that the high sheriff had arrived.

Handing the laser tool to his foreman, he said, "Take over, Mitch, and make sure you keep Harv digging at the right level. I'll be back in a few minutes."

Jared climbed out of the ditch and walked over to where Bram had parked his pickup truck in an out-of-the-way spot at the edge of the work site.

"What's up?" he called to his brother.

The lazy smile on Bram's face as he climbed out of the vehicle quickly assured Jared that the sheriff's early visit had nothing to do with an emergency.

"I've been sent on a mission," Bram said.

Jared casually propped his boot on the pickup bumper. "Well, from the way you're grinning it must not be a dangerous one."

Bram chuckled. "I don't know yet. Depends on whether you want to be stubborn about this."

Jared's brows lifted in surprise. "Me? What do I have to do with anything?"

Bram slanted him a mocking look. "Oh come on, Jared. You're Black Arrow's newest hero. And the mayor has sent me out here to fetch you to his office. He wants to present you with a key to the city. And I wouldn't be a bit surprised if he and the city council vote to change the name of Main Street to Jared Colton Boulevard," he added dryly.

Willow had already warned Jared that the mayor had been trying to contact him. But he still found it hard to believe that a city politician wanted anything to do with him. For the past ten years Jared had spent most of his time away from Black Arrow and before then he'd never been a civic-minded citizen. He'd mostly been a hell-raiser and womanizer. The idea that the mayor, or anyone else for that matter, saw him in a heroic light was almost laughable.

Shaking his head with disbelief, Jared said, "Don't tell me the press is going to be there."

Bram grunted with amusement. "It's election year. The mayor is hardly going to pass up a chance to get his photo in the paper. Especially when it's connected to a happy story. And I've already had a call from someone in Oklahoma City saying AP has picked up your story and published it in the *Daily*. So I don't look for this thing to die down soon."

Jared frowned and heaved out a heavy breath. "Not when the public officials around here want to keep feeding it."

"Humor me, brother," Bram told him. "Since the mayor wants me to join in on the ceremony, too, I can hardly go back and tell him you don't want a key to the city. I do have to get along with the man."

With another shake of his head, Jared said, "Don't get me wrong, Bram, I appreciate the mayor's gesture. But if this hero stuff keeps up, it's going to start getting embarrassing." And for some reason it was important that he didn't come across to Kerry as a showoff. He'd worked hard to rescue Peggy because he'd desperately wanted to save the little girl's life. Not to make himself out a hero.

"Since when did you get so humble, little brother?" Bram asked wryly. "You've always loved the spotlight. Especially when it caused the females to flock around you."

Pulling his boot from the bumper, Jared hooked his

thumbs over his belt and looked out over the busy work site. The morning sun was already warming a bright blue sky and beyond the heavy equipment and the scars they had made in the earth, deep green grass and fully leafed trees announced the rebirth of spring. It was going to be a glorious day and Jared had never felt more glad to be alive and to be back in Black Arrow.

"You make me sound like some rooster calling for a bunch of hens to gather around him."

Bram chuckled. "Well, you are, aren't you?"

Jared turned his gaze back to his brother. "Why no," he said with faint surprise. "Those days are long gone, Bram."

Bram stared at Jared as though he was a thief caught in the act, yet still trying to plead his innocence. "What in hell has come over you? You've been a terror to women since you were eight years old. You'd have to be dead to give up on them now."

Shrugging, Jared folded his arms across his chest and glanced evasively back to the spot where his foreman was directing a backhoe operator. No matter where he looked he saw Kerry's luminous brown eyes and soft gentle lips. It had been that way with him ever since he'd pulled Peggy out of the crumbling pipe and placed her in Kerry's arms. He didn't understand why or how such a quiet, unassuming woman had captured his thoughts so completely. But she had. And he wasn't at all sure how he was going to cure himself.

"I didn't say I was giving up on women entirely," he said to Bram. "I just meant—well, I'm thirty-four years old. I'm bored with all that playing around I used to do."

Bram studied his brother through squinted eyes. "All right," he said finally, "who is she?"

Jared's look of surprise was followed by a laugh that was full of denial. "There is no she. Yet," he added, then quickly deciding it was high time to change the subject, he slapped an affectionate hand on Bram's shoulder. "Now tell me about this thing with the mayor. When do I have to be there?"

Bram glanced at his watch. "About thirty minutes. So hop in and give me the honor of driving Black Arrow's hero into town."

Seeing there wasn't anyway he could disappoint his brother, Jared said, "All right, you don't have to drag out your handcuffs. I'll go. Just let me go tell the foreman what's going on."

Enola stared moodily at the television set as Kerry watched out the front door for Jared's arrival.

"You know I am not happy about this, Kerry."

Careful to keep her sigh silent, she said, "Yes, Mom. I can see that I've disappointed you by choosing to have dinner with Jared."

Tight-lipped, Enola turned her gaze on her daughter. "It's not the dinner—it's the idea that you want to spend time with this man."

"Yes, I do want to spend time with Jared," she conceded. "He's been very nice to me. And Peggy adores him."

Enola turned her gaze back to the television, but Kerry knew her mother couldn't have told anyone what was flickering across the screen. The woman was silently seething.

"That's because he knows exactly how to charm women. Mark my words, you and Peggy will both be hurt if this carries on much further."

The way you were hurt, Kerry wanted to say. But

she didn't. Pointing out her mother's miserable marriage wouldn't help matters now.

"Mom, it's been nearly four years since I've had a man in my life. That's a long time and I'm still a young woman. I don't want to bury myself forever."

Enola shot her an accusing look. "How many times have I tried to get you to go out? I could probably think of ten young men in the past year that you could have dated. But no. You always found excuses not to go."

Kerry tried her best not to bristle. Maybe she had made a mistake with Damon, but she was her own person. Good or bad, she had to make her own choices. "I wasn't attracted to any of those men, Mom. There wasn't one of them I would have felt comfortable going on a date with."

Her remarks brought Enola to her feet. "So you're telling me that you find Jared Colton attractive? That you feel comfortable with him?" she asked in an astounded voice. "Kerry, the man is up to no good. He's only going to use you and hurt Peggy in the process."

Amazed at how desperate she was to see Jared arrive, Kerry kept her eyes focused on the driveway. "All men aren't users, Mom. And did you ever stop to think that Jared might want to spend time with me because he actually likes me? Or have you decided that the only reason a man would pay attention to me is to get me in bed?"

Enola gasped with outrage. "That's a filthy remark."

Kerry made a pleading gesture with her hand. "Look, Mom. Damon crushed my self-worth. For a long time I didn't think much of myself. And I didn't think anyone else did either, especially men. But I've tried to put all that past me. It lifts my spirits to think that Jared might see something special in me. Something more than just a one-night stand. Surely you can understand that.''

Enola shook her head. ''Jared Colton sees all women as objects and the sooner you realize that, the better.''

With that her mother stormed out of the room and Kerry let out a weary sigh. All afternoon, she'd been asking herself if she was crazy to agree to this dinner date with Jared. Even this evening, while she'd been dressing, she'd still been doubting the wisdom of her decision to go. But that had all changed the moment Enola had ripped into her.

Being in Jared's company might be worse than playing with fire. But she was tired of living behind the shelter of her mother's apron.

''Mama, when is Jared coming?''

Peggy's voice broke into Kerry's thoughts and she looked around at the angelic sight of her daughter all dressed up in a red sundress and white sandals. Claws was carefully cradled in one arm and the sight of the little orange cat made her soft smile deepen. Jared had chosen the perfect pet for her daughter. In spite of the endless, sometimes pestering attention Peggy gave the cat, the little guy never hissed or clawed. He seemed to understand that Peggy loved him and he returned her affection with purrs and licks from his spiky tongue.

''Any minute now, darlin'. Are you ready to go?''

Peggy grinned and hopped on her toes. ''Yeah! I want Jared to carry me.''

''Carry you?'' Kerry asked with a puzzled smile. ''You're a big girl now. You don't need to be carried.''

Peggy giggled and the tinkling, musical sound reassured Kerry that her daughter was slowly returning to normal.

"I know. But Jared smells good. And he's big and strong."

When a three-year-old noticed such things, there was no way a grown woman could ignore them, she thought wryly. But she had to try. She couldn't let herself fall victim to Jared's charms. If she did, she would lose her head and then her heart.

Twenty minutes later, the three of them were seated in the booth of a popular downtown steakhouse. To no surprise of Kerry's, her daughter had chosen to sit in a booster seat placed next to Jared and so far the child had dominated the conversation.

As of yet, Kerry had not interfered with the interplay going back and forth between Jared and her daughter. Instead of giving him a break, she'd purposely allowed Peggy to chatter on. Which was mean of her, she supposed. Especially when she knew Jared wasn't accustomed to entertaining small children.

Yet these past few minutes had given her a chance to study the man sitting across from her, to watch for any sign that he resented Peggy's presence. But so far he'd displayed nothing but patience and genuine fondness for her daughter. That in itself was enough to soften Kerry's heart toward him.

"Peggy, you're about to talk Jared's ear off. He'll have to get it sewn back on." She finally spoke up.

Chuckling, Jared reached up and tugged his ear that was receiving the brunt of Peggy's chatter. "Your mama is teasing, little dove. My ear is still hooked on pretty tight."

As though she needed to confirm things for herself, Peggy reached up and touched Jared's ear, then shot her mother a quizzical look.

"His ear is okay, Mama. It's not gonna fall off."

Kerry laughed softly. "I was only teasing, Peggy."

"That means you can talk all you want to," Jared said to Peggy as he reached over and gently tweaked her rosy brown cheek.

The playful gesture was natural and full of affection and Kerry couldn't help but imagine what it would be like for Peggy to have this man as her father. Seeing him like this with her daughter made Kerry believe he would be a wonderful, caring father. But would he always be there to love her and support her, even after she'd grown into womanhood? she wondered. Or would the role of father and husband be boring to him after years of playing the field?

Thankfully the waitress suddenly appeared with their orders and scattered Kerry's wandering thoughts. The meal wound up being far more relaxed and enjoyable than she'd expected. When Jared eventually suggested it was time for them to leave, she was actually disappointed.

"Of course," Kerry told him as the three of them left the booth. "Don't let us keep you out late. Especially when you have work tomorrow."

Amused by her sudden jump to conclusions, he gave her a crooked grin. "I didn't mean that we needed to go home now. I have something else planned for the two of you."

Feeling a bit like a foolish teenager on a first date, her heart lifted with excitement. "Oh? What is it?"

"I thought you might want to have a little visit with Great-grandfather George," he answered as the three

of them made their way toward the exit of the building.
"I've already told him about you and Peggy and I
know he'd enjoy meeting the two of you."

Kerry studied his face and as she did the corners of
her lips tilted to a faint smile. If Jared Colton was nothing but a playboy, he was doing a good job of masking
it. She said, "I guess you realize that you're not living
up to your reputation."

Grinning, he snapped his fingers in a gesture of regret. "Dang, I must be losing my touch."

No. He wasn't losing his touch, Kerry thought. She
was falling for his masculine charms hook, line and
sinker. But she'd worry about that later. Tonight she
was simply going to enjoy herself. And him.

The smile on her face deepened. "If that's the case,
then Peggy and I would be happy to visit your great-
grandfather."

Chapter Six

About forty minutes later the three of them drove down a narrow dirt lane until they came to the small house where George "Nahiman" WhiteBear lived. Built just before the Great Depression and dust bowl had devastated Oklahoma, the structure was covered with brown tar siding made to look like mortared rock. A shallow porch ran across the narrow front and was totally shaded by an enormous cottonwood tree that grew on the west side of the tiny yard.

They found the old man sitting in a wooden rocker on the porch. Nearby, a carved cane of native cedar was worn smooth from years of use. As Kerry drew closer, she decided that George had to be somewhere in his mid-nineties and appeared to be amazingly alert for his advancing years. His sharp, hawklike features were dark brown and lined with a network of endless wrinkles. Black eyes were partially hidden by drooping folds of skin, while coarse, gray hair was slicked back from his face and fell to his shoulders. He wore black jeans, a white shirt and a black vest patterned with beaded shapes of horses and bears. Soft brown moccasins covered his otherwise bare feet.

"Great-grandfather, this is Kerry WindWalker and her daughter Peggy," Jared said.

The old Comanche lifted a gnarled hand adorned with a large silver ring that was set with smooth stones of turquoise and malachite. Kerry clasped the bony fingers and smiled with genuine pleasure.

"It's an honor to meet you, Mr. WhiteBear."

George cast Jared a look that said he was already impressed with Kerry's gracious manners. To Kerry he said, "I have already heard a lot about you and the little dove who was lost. I'm glad my grandson was able to save her life."

She glanced up at Peggy who was perfectly content with her perch on Jared's strong arm. "I'm very glad, too, Mr. WhiteBear."

The old man's head shook back and forth. "Call me George," he said to her. "Mr. WhiteBear makes me sound like an old man."

Jared laughed. "You are old, Great-grandfather. There's no use trying to make Kerry believe otherwise. And don't go making eyes at her either 'cause she's my girl."

To emphasize his point, he curled his free arm around Kerry's shoulders. A few days ago, the intimate gesture would have sent her into a silent panic. But tonight was different. She was beginning to trust Jared enough to relax. And his touch made her feel special and protected. Two things she'd never expected to feel again in her life.

Jared set Peggy on her feet and the child immediately scurried to the opposite end of the porch and sat down cross-legged on the floor. Since no other chairs were available, Kerry took a seat beside Jared in a nearby wooden porch swing.

George inclined his head at the two adults and grinned. Except for an empty gap where an eyetooth used to be, his teeth were incredibly straight and white.

"You have liked many women, my grandson. But I think this is the woman our Great Spirit has made for you."

For as long as Jared could remember, George had been spouting off words of wisdom and predictions of things to come. Especially where family members were concerned. But Jared had never paid too much attention to Great-grandfather's remarks. The mystic lore of his Comanche heritage had never figured into his busy modern life. Yet this particular divination sent a strange shiver down his spine. Just because he wanted to spend a little time with Kerry didn't mean he was looking for a wife!

He turned his head slightly toward Kerry to see that she was studying him with raised eyebrows. No doubt she'd latched on to George's remark about his grandson's many women. Damn it. The old man could have kept that to himself.

"He's exaggerating about the women," Jared whispered. "You're the first woman I've ever brought out here to meet him."

Kerry didn't know whether to feel flattered or worried. She'd believed Jared had brought her out here to his great-grandfather's place because he'd thought she would enjoy meeting the old Comanche man. But now he seemed to be hinting there was a more intimate meaning behind this visit. And what had George meant by the Great Spirit making her for Jared? she wondered. Did he really believe God intended the two of them to be together?

Don't be crazy, Kerry. Jared Colton has no long-term interest in you. He's only enjoying your company while he's here in Black Arrow. George WhiteBear was a very old man. He probably didn't know half of what he was saying.

Seeing the unsettled look on Kerry's face, Jared decided it would be best to change the subject completely.

"How have you been, Great-grandfather?" he asked. "Have your knees been giving you trouble?"

George rested long bony hands on both knees. "I walked a mile yesterday with Betty. The old woman says all I need is a good limbering up."

"She's probably right," Jared agreed with a chuckle, then explained to Kerry, "Betty is an eighty-year-old woman who lives down the street from my sister's feed store. She's had a crush on Great-grandfather for years now. But he refuses to give in and marry her."

"Apparently bachelorhood runs in your family," she said with wry amusement.

He flashed her a guilty grin before he turned his attention back to his great-grandfather. "Well, did the walk limber up your knees?"

George WhiteBear cackled with glee. "Guess the old woman was right. Today my knees feel as good as they did when I was seventy. Maybe I ought to give the old woman a kiss. What do you think about that?" he asked Jared.

"I think you're going to mess around and get yourself in real trouble with Betty. She might be more woman than you can handle.''

George's chest swelled as he waved away his great-grandson's suggestion. ''Bull. I'm a Comanche warrior. I could still ride these plains and fight off the Kiowas if I had to.''

''Yeah, but I think Betty has the idea you're a big chief. I wonder where she came up with a notion like that?'' Jared asked, then shared a covert wink with Kerry.

''Well,'' George said with a sheepish shrug, ''the woman thinks she knows nobility when she sees it and I didn't want to make her out as a liar.''

Jared laughed loudly and Kerry could plainly see he adored his great-grandfather.

''Naw,'' Jared agreed with George, ''that wouldn't have been a gentlemanly thing to do.''

Suddenly George grabbed up his cane and slowly pushed himself to his feet. When he turned and walked over to where Peggy still sat, the little girl quietly studied him with wide, fascinated eyes.

''Come with me, Chenoa,'' he invited with a gentle pat on top of her head. ''I'll show you my chickens and horses. I might even let you gather the eggs. Would you like that?''

After regarding him for a moment, Peggy gave him a slow, thoughtful nod, then looked to her mother for permission.

Kerry said, ''Stay close to George. And do what he tells you to do.''

''I will, Mama,'' she promised.

After George and her daughter had left the porch and disappeared around the side of the house, Kerry said, ''I'm surprised. Peggy doesn't normally take to men.

Except for you,'' she added wryly. ''But she seems to feel comfortable with your great-grandfather.''

''Charming women runs in the family,'' Jared teased, then with a contented sigh, he pushed the toe of his boot against the floor and put the swing in gentle motion. ''Actually, I don't know of any kid that doesn't like George. Maybe that's because even though he's in his nineties, he still has the heart of a young boy.''

The fiery ball of evening sun had finally fallen, lengthening the shadows across the porch and the fresh-mown grass. Out near the wire fence that separated the small yard from the nearby woods, a two-story martin house was covered with the small purplish birds. Their happy songs were joined in by the high-pitched drone of cicadas inhabiting the cottonwood and the occasional call of a tree frog. The summer sounds and the velvety warm air wrapped around Kerry like the welcome arms of a lover.

''Exactly how old is George?'' she asked him.

''No one really knows for certain. I don't believe he ever had an original birth certificate. He claims he's ninety-seven and Gloria, our grandmother, believes he was born well before statehood in nineteen-seven. So we figure he has to be in his upper nineties for sure.''

Kerry was amazed. ''Oh my. That means he was a baby when this land was still Oklahoma Territory. There was no law to speak of and every bandit and gunslinger in the West came here to evade jail or the end of a rope. It's incredible to think that anyone from that era is still living, much less be as spry and alert as George.''

His gray eyes sparkled as he studied her face. ''You make his life sound fascinating.''

Her widened eyes said she found his remark incredible. "His life is fascinating. He's seen decades of history."

One corner of his lips crooked upward in an expression of guilt. "Well, I'm not exactly a history buff, Kerry. And George has spent his whole life here in Comanche County. He's not what you'd call world educated."

"You don't have to see the world in order to be wise about life, Jared."

Funny that this beautiful young woman would say the very same thing to him that George had said to him more than twelve years ago when he'd first left Black Arrow to spread his wings. At the time Jared had considered living in a quiet Oklahoma town as not really living. And down through the years he'd stayed away from Black Arrow far more than he'd visited. But now he was beginning to wonder if he'd been missing out on things he'd once taken for granted.

"Well, some people around town might debate whether George is wise or not. But one thing is for sure, he's never been bashful about letting any of his relatives know when he thought they were doing wrong."

She sighed wistfully. "Like I told you the other night, you're a lucky man, Jared. You have such a sense of family. I've never had anyone but Mom," she admitted. "And Peggy, of course."

"What about your father? Is he not around anymore?"

With a shake of her head, Kerry looked away from him and focused her gaze on the shadows stretching across the opposite end of the porch. "No. Marvin passed away a few years ago. But he was someone I hardly knew. After I was born my parents drifted apart.

Dad would wander in and out of our lives when we least expected it. Sometimes he'd be gone for months, other times he might return after a few days. I've tried to think of a time I saw him when he wasn't drinking. But I can't. And I used to wonder if I was the reason he drank. Because he didn't want the responsibility of a child. But after he died...well, I gave up trying to figure him out."

The sad regret Jared saw on her face suddenly had him thinking back to all the happy times he and his brothers had shared with their dad while fishing on Lake Waurika, hunting pheasant up in the panhandle or just tossing the football in the back yard. Trevor Colton had loved his children and even though he'd been a hardworking man, he'd always made time to give each of them attention.

For a long time after his father's death, Jared had been bitter and angry that someone he'd loved and needed so much had been taken from him. But now he could see that Kerry was right. He was lucky. He'd had a loving father and he had years of wonderful memories of a man who'd spent his whole life making things as good as he could for his wife and children. That was much more than Kerry would ever have. And the realization tore at him.

"Your mother never remarried after Marvin died?"

Kerry shook her head. "She runs if a man so much as looks in her direction. And if one does manage to corner her, she isn't bashful about setting him straight about her feelings."

He nodded. "She sounds like my Grandmother Gloria. George has often tried to get her to marry, but being widowed at a young age must have twisted her.

She doesn't have any interest in becoming a wife again.''

Curious, Kerry asked, ''Did your dad and his twin brother ever know their father? Or did he die before they were old enough to remember?''

''From what I understand none of the family ever met the man. Back in nineteen-forty Gloria left here and went to Reno, Nevada. She was working as a cocktail waitress when she met and married my grandfather. By the time she finally came back here to Black Arrow, she was pregnant with twins and her husband had been killed in some sort of accident.''

''How tragic,'' Kerry murmured. ''She must have never gotten over her first love.''

Her remark had Jared curiously studying her face and after a moment he reached over and picked up her hand. ''Is that what happened to you? You've never gotten over Peggy's father?''

Surprise parted her lips and then her heart lurched into a heavy thud. ''What—makes you ask that?''

His gray eyes continued to roam her face and she felt her cheeks warming to their touch. He was so close his thigh was brushing against hers and his masculine scent was swirling around her like a seductive cloak. She'd never been so aware of a man or so reminded that she was a woman. A woman who'd not been caressed or kissed in nearly four long years.

''You told me you don't date,'' he reasoned. ''Peggy is three years old. Most women would have gotten over losing a lover by that time.''

A lover. How strange that term seemed in connection with Damon. At one time Kerry had considered him the very light of her life. Yet now she had to look back on that time in Virginia and wonder if what she'd felt had been infatuation for him and the idea of having a family of her own.

"Peggy's father is...truly out of our lives."

The relief Jared felt was so great it almost seemed indecent. He shouldn't be glad that Peggy's father was out of the picture. The child deserved two loving parents. Yet he was happy, very happy that Kerry was free for the taking.

"I can't imagine any man not wanting to be involved in his daughter's life," Jared said. "Especially one like little Peggy. She's bright and beautiful and loving."

Kerry found herself squeezing his fingers in response to his kind words. "Damon doesn't even know what sex his child is, much less that she's a lovely little girl. He doesn't want to know."

"Do you...ever try to contact him?"

Her mocking snort was full of bitterness. "No. Even if I did, he wouldn't respond. You see, Damon Whitfield is from an old, respected family in South Carolina. He'd rather die than let his friends or relatives know that he fathered the child of a Comanche Indian."

Jared put down the toe of his boot and the gentle sway of the swing stopped so abruptly she teetered forward.

"Kerry, are you telling me that you're a single mother because some man didn't think you were good enough to be his wife?"

Embarrassed heat poured into her cheeks and she quickly looked away from his probing gray eyes.

"I don't know why you sound surprised," she said with a sigh. "You're a Comanche, or at least part Comanche. You, more than anyone ought to know we're not always looked upon as regular folks."

Jared let out a loud groan of protest. "That sort of

racial thinking went out ages ago. Once in a great while, I might hear a crude comment made about redskins or savages. But it's usually uttered by some nasty drunk in a bar or an illiterate redneck that doesn't know any better.''

Before Jared had picked her and Peggy up this evening, she'd worried about keeping her distance from this man. And not just in a physical sense, but in an emotional way, too. She'd wanted their dinner date to be enjoyable but safely detached. Yet now that she was sitting here beside Jared in the waning twilight and his warm hand was closed protectively around hers, it felt natural, even right to be sharing a part of her life with him.

''That's usually true, Jared. And I guess you're wondering what I was doing with a guy like that in the first place. But believe me, I didn't know about Damon's real feelings until it was too late.''

Jared glanced briefly over his shoulder. Now that he had Kerry talking, he hoped his great-grandfather would keep Peggy out at the brooder house long enough for him to find out the reason for her broken heart.

''Where did you meet him? In college?''

She nodded. ''He was in his final year at the University of Virginia and I was working on my master's.'' She paused and the tightness of her features told Jared that relaying her past to him was like digging into a festering wound.

''I have to admit that I was naive,'' she went on. ''Before I met Damon, I'd never had a steady boyfriend. I guess the misery I'd watched my mother go through with Marvin made me leery of getting involved with anyone. But Damon was persistent. And he was white. For some idiotic reason, I thought that made him safe. I thought there wasn't any way he could be like my father. But in actuality he was worse.''

''What do you mean by that?'' Jared asked. From what he remembered of Marvin WindWalker, the man had been a worthless drunk. As far as Jared could see, the only redeeming quality he'd had was having a daughter like Kerry.

Pushed by the painful memories crowding into her mind, Kerry rose from the swing and walked to the opposite end of the porch. A moment later, as she leaned against one of the wooden posts that supported the roof, she felt Jared's hand close over her shoulder.

Drawing in a bracing breath, she said, ''This is hard to talk about, Jared. It's hard to admit to anyone that I was such a fool.''

''Kerry,'' he whispered gently. ''Don't call yourself a fool. That's not true.''

As she looked up at him something hard and painful snapped inside her and the release was so great she lay her head against his chest. ''Oh Jared,'' she said softly, ''I never stopped to think that Damon was just using me. That he only wanted my body. He had a glib tongue and I believed him when he said he wanted to marry me once he finished his college studies. I believed all the wonderful plans he made for the two of us.''

The feel of her cheek nestled against him was one of the sweetest sensations he could ever remember and the gesture of trust evoked a sudden fierce longing to protect this woman in a way Jared had never felt before.

Softly, carefully, he stroked the back of her hair. ''So what happened? You got pregnant and he left you?''

"Not exactly," she murmured. "After a time both of us began to realize we wanted different things in life and those differences caused all sort of arguments and problems. By the time I discovered I was pregnant, we'd already ended our relationship. But I wanted my child and I thought Damon would, too. I believed he would care enough to work out our differences and that he would want to get married for the sake of the baby."

Jared had always considered himself fortunate that none of his former girlfriends had approached him with the news that he was going to be a daddy. But then he'd always been very careful not to get a woman or himself in such a predicament. Which hadn't been all that hard considering his relationships were purposely kept to a short-term basis. Yet now that he'd heard Kerry's story, he knew that he could never walk away from a child. Even if he didn't truly love the mother.

"So this guy didn't want to get married?" Jared asked.

She made a strangled sound that was intended to be a mocking laugh. "Not hardly. He made it plain that he'd had other plans all along and that I would have never fit into his social circles back in South Carolina."

The intense rage Jared felt toward the man who'd betrayed Kerry took him by surprise. "He must have been a real bastard."

Her eyes shadowed with the past, Kerry lifted her head to look at him. "His duplicity is what really jolted me, Jared. It was so hard to believe that the man I'd known was all just an act on his part. Then on top of that, I had to face the fact that I was so gullible, so dumb that I hadn't seen through him."

Shaking his head, he reached out and cupped his hand against her cheek. "You weren't dumb. You had a gentle, trusting heart and the man took advantage of it. I'd like to get my hands on him for about ten minutes. He'd be eating out of a straw for a few months. Then maybe he'd think twice about treating some other woman the way he treated you.''

The fact that he wanted to avenge the hurt she'd been put through thrilled her. She'd never had a father, brother or any man take up for her in such a gallant way and it made her feel protected and very feminine.

Rising up on her toes, she pressed a brief kiss against his cheek. "Thank you for the thought, Jared. And for caring.''

He did care, he realized. Far more than she could guess and way more than he'd ever intended.

"I do care,'' he murmured, then before she could pull away completely, he wrapped his arms around her shoulders and lowered his mouth to hers.

Instinctively, her eyelids fluttered downward. Her heart seemed to quit beating, the air in her lungs grew stale and her mind refused to think about anything except the sudden sweep of sensations through her body.

Beneath his hands he felt her muscles tense like a skittish colt and he told himself to keep the kiss light and short. But the taste of her lips was too sweet, too tempting to resist. Before he realized what he was doing, he was drawing her closer and slanting his mouth over hers hungrily.

Kerry was quickly losing her sanity and she silently screamed at herself to tear her mouth from his, to leave the seductive circle of his arms. But the pleasure of being this close to him was stronger than her common sense.

Thankfully, only a few more moments passed before

the approaching sound of George's voice tore the two of them apart.

Embarrassed by her reckless behavior, Kerry quickly turned her back to Jared and gripped the porch post to steady her shaky legs.

Behind her, Jared reached out to touch her shoulder. "Kerry."

The hoarse whisper of her name suggested to Kerry that he'd been just as affected by their kiss as she'd been. But then she was hardly in any shape to gauge her own reaction, much less his. Besides, he'd had all kinds of practice with women, she told herself. He probably knew just what to say, just how to sound to make himself seem sincere.

"Don't say anything, Jared," she quietly pleaded. "It's too embarrassing."

"Embarrassing!" he repeated in a loud, insulted tone. Then seeing that George and Peggy were now climbing the steps, he lowered his voice for Kerry's ears only. "I didn't feel anything embarrassing about kissing you!"

Seeing that he'd misinterpreted her remark, she whirled back to face him, then inwardly groaned as her eyes connected with his dark, striking features. The man was simply too good to look at and definitely too good to kiss.

"That's not what I meant. I—I'm ashamed at my behavior. I should have—never kissed you like that. Now you're probably thinking I'm not a lady."

Even though George and Peggy had now returned to the porch, Jared laughed with pure pleasure and caressed her cheek in an extremely intimate way.

"Honey, you'd be surprised at what I'm thinking about you."

Chapter Seven

The next afternoon Kerry carried a stack of completed promissory notes into Clarence's office for his signature and found the older man quietly reading the newspaper.

"Is that all you have to do around this place?" she teased.

He looked up questioningly and smiled the moment he realized the intruder in his office was Kerry.

"Work, work, work," he bantered back at her. "You won't even give a man five minutes to read the newspaper."

She smiled. "I only need your signature on a few things before I file them away."

"No problem." He placed the paper to one side of his desk and reached to take the load of documents from Kerry's arms.

As she handed them over, her eye caught the large

photo on the front page of the local paper. Even from an upside-down position, she identified one of the men as Jared.

"I'm finished with the paper if you'd like to read it," Clarence said as he began to scrawl his name across the bottom of a typed page.

Unaware that she'd been craning her neck for a better look, Kerry frowned at him. "Why would I want to read the newspaper? I have work to do."

"Then why are you breaking your neck to see that picture of the Coltons?" He handed the paper up to her. "Here. Take a look while I finish signing these notes."

Knowing it would look foolish to argue, Kerry took the newspaper and eased down in the chair situated in front of Clarence's desk. As she scanned the photo of Jared accepting a huge key from the mayor of Black Arrow, Clarence said, "Looks like the Coltons have really made a splash in this town."

"I wouldn't call two newspaper articles making a big splash," Kerry countered, while wondering why Jared hadn't mentioned this meeting with the mayor to her last night. Maybe he hadn't considered it a big deal, but she did. Especially when the whole incident was connected to her daughter.

"From what I hear, the news of Jared saving little Peggy has hit the *Daily Oklahoman* and the *Tulsa World*. And this morning while I was over in the courthouse building, Hazel tells me that someone was in there yesterday digging up more information on the Coltons."

A quizzical frown wrinkled Kerry's forehead as she looked up from the paper. "In the courthouse? There wouldn't be any sort of information there about Peggy's rescue. Who was this person?''

Clarence shrugged. ''Some man she'd never seen before. She didn't think he was from this area. Must have been some reporter.''

''Must have been,'' Kerry murmured thoughtfully. ''What sort of information was this person wanting?''

Clarence put down his pen and propped his elbows on his desk. ''Hazel said he wanted genealogical information on Gloria and all of her descendants.''

''That's odd,'' Kerry mused aloud. ''If he wanted that sort of information all he had to do was go to the sheriff's department and visit with Bram. He's the oldest of both the Colton families. He probably knows more about the family tree than most of the younger members. Or better yet, he could have talked to Gloria herself.''

''Oh, I wouldn't call it weird, Kerry. Jared has been in the spotlight for the past few days and people all over the state are reading about him. Someone probably wants to do a story on him and his family. That's all.''

Clarence could be right, Kerry thought. But something about the whole thing didn't ring true with her.

''If that's the case, he should have interviewed Jared personally. That's the normal way to gather information.''

''Maybe he did,'' Clarence suggested.

Kerry immediately shook her head. ''No. He couldn't have. I—''

She stopped so abruptly that Clarence immediately raised his eyebrows and prodded her to continue. ''You what?'' he asked.

Rosy color tinged Kerry's cheeks as she quickly stood and placed the newspaper back on his desk.

Spending time with Jared was not necessarily something she needed to keep secret. But Clarence was the closest thing she had to a father and she wasn't ready to hear a lecture from him about dating a playboy. She'd already gotten enough of that from her mother.

"Well, I just—happened to be with Jared last night," she explained. "And he didn't mention anything about this stranger at the courthouse."

Clarence leaned back in his chair and studied her with wry speculation. "I wasn't aware that you were that well acquainted with Jared Colton."

Kerry's shrug was more of an effort to appear casual than anything else. "Gloria Colton and her father, George, were living here long before I was born. And many of her grandchildren are around my own age. We went to school together. The Coltons are a well-known family in Black Arrow. Especially with Bram being the sheriff and Gray a judge."

"That's true," Clarence agreed. "But from what I understand, Jared hasn't been a homebody. He's been gone from here for the past ten or twelve years. And he is quite a bit older than you."

Kerry leveled an annoyed look at him. "Aren't you jumping to conclusions, Clarence? Just because I was with the man last night doesn't mean there's anything serious going on between us."

Chuckling, he held up both hands in a gesture of innocence. "Whoa. I'm not jumping to anything. I was just a little surprised, that's all. You've worked here for three years and I've never known you to date anyone."

Clarence made it sound as though she'd suddenly taken a major turn in her life. And it wasn't that way, she thought. She couldn't let it be that way. Jared's kiss might have turned her inside out, but he wasn't a man she could let herself get serious about.

"Jared and I aren't—exactly dating. He's—been helping me with Peggy. She was so traumatized after her ordeal that she would hardly talk, much less eat. But she trusts Jared. And since he's been spending time with her, she's getting right back to her old self."

A sly smile creased the older man's face. "So this is not a case of like daughter, like mother."

"Not at all," Kerry said, then turned and headed out of the room before he could say anymore about her connection with Jared.

"Uh, Kerry," Clarence called to her. "Aren't you forgetting something?"

She paused at the door to glance questioningly back at him.

"I've signed all the notes," he said, inclining his head toward the stack of papers she'd carried to him only minutes earlier. "Don't you want to file them?"

Red-faced now, Kerry hurried back to his desk and snatched up the stack of documents. "Everyone gets distracted now and then," she explained.

Clarence grinned at her. "Yeah, we do. And I'm very glad to finally see that you haven't forgotten you're a woman."

If Kerry had forgotten, Jared had suddenly reminded her last night with that tantalizing kiss. Now she was going around as though she was moonstruck. She had to snap out of it before she did something foolish, something that might not only break her heart, but her daughter's heart, too.

"I'm a mother first, Clarence. Always."

* * *

That evening when Kerry arrived home from work, she found the house quiet and a note from her mother saying she and Peggy had gone to visit a friend over at Indiahoma and wouldn't be back until later that evening.

After changing into a pair of jean shorts and a white sleeveless blouse, she made herself a sandwich and a glass of iced tea and carried the whole lot out to the porch to eat her solitary supper. As she ate, Kerry continued to ponder over the talk that a stranger had been at the courthouse digging into the Colton family records. The whole idea still struck her as odd and she wondered if Jared or any of the Coltons knew about the stranger.

It's none of your business, Kerry. You don't need to use this as an excuse to see Jared again. Being in the man's company isn't healthy for your heart or your head.

Okay, she conceded to the little voice of common sense. If seeing Jared was a bad idea, she could call Jared's younger sister, Willow. But she hadn't spoken to Willow in ages. Calling her up out of the blue and relaying such an odd story would have the woman thinking Kerry was crazy.

Of course, there was another option to consider. Bram was the sheriff. He was the man who needed to be alerted to suspicious goings on. But right now Kerry only had hearsay and she didn't want to bother a busy sheriff with something that might turn out to be nothing more than gossip.

No, going to Jared and telling him about the stranger would be far easier. Then she could leave it up to him as to whether Bram or the rest of the family should be told. With that final reasoning, she stepped off the porch and walked around to the side of the house where the yard opened up and she could see beyond the houses and trees to the work site where Peggy had been trapped.

From this angle she could see the movement of heavy machinery and several men at work on the ground. At this distance it was impossible to tell if one of them was Jared, but she was fairly certain his white pickup truck was among the vehicles parked nearby.

With sudden decision, she went back into the house and left a note that she'd gone for a walk. Then after a quick brush through her hair and a dab of cherry-red lipstick, she set off for Jared's work site.

A few minutes later Jared spotted her slim figure picking her way over the uneven ground. The sight of her stunned him. Even though she'd kissed him last night like she'd enjoyed it, he'd not expected her to visit him on her own accord. The idea that she might actually want to see him filled him with warm pleasure.

Pulling off his hard hat, he walked out to meet her.

"Hello," he greeted with a broad smile. "This is a nice surprise."

Kerry felt a blush sting her cheeks as she tried to keep the memory of their kiss at bay. But it was impossible to do when just looking at his lips sent a curl of excitement spiraling through her.

"Hello," she said, then quickly asked, "Do you have a minute or two? Or did I come at a bad time?"

He ran a hand through the sweaty hair plastered to his forehead. "No time is a bad time for you, Kerry."

The suggestive gleam in his eyes caused her breath to hang in her throat. When she did finally speak, she sounded as though she'd just run from the WindWalker house rather than walk. "Well, I know I'm disturbing you. But I had something on my mind that couldn't wait.''

The smile on his face deepened to a sexy grin. ''I hope the something is me.''

She tried to keep a stern face, but the joy at seeing him again was radiating through her like a golden sun-ray and tilting the corners of her lips. ''Have you always liked to tease?'' she asked.

''Who said I was teasing?'' he asked with a chuckle, then without explaining his intentions he took her by the arm and led her over to a shady spot where his truck was parked. After he let down the tailgate, he placed his hands on her waist and lifted her up to the makeshift seat.

Kerry's heart was pounding by the time he joined her on the tailgate, yet she tried her best to remain calm and collected. A task made even more difficult by the fact that he made denim work clothes and muddy boots look so sexy it felt like a downright sin just to look at him.

''Jared,'' she began with a tone of gentle warning, ''I don't want you to start getting any ideas about— that kiss last night. That's not the reason I'm here.''

He feigned such a look of disappointment, she laughed before she could stop herself.

''How can you laugh?'' he asked. ''I'm hurt. Deeply hurt that you didn't walk all the way out here to get a kiss from me.''

She rolled her eyes at his nonsense, then squealed with shock as he suddenly snatched a hold on her shoulders and tugged her up against his chest.

''Jared! What—''

The leisurely kiss he planted on her lips stopped her

words and took her breath away. By the time he finally pulled his head back, she was sputtering for air.

"I didn't come out here to put on a show for your crew either!"

His soft laughter fanned her ear. "The crew can't see us from here."

Kerry twisted around so that she was looking back in the direction of the work site. Thankfully, he was right. The two of them were hidden by the cab of the truck and the bulk of the vehicle parked next to them.

"That's beside the point," she said as she managed to squirm out of his arms and scoot to the very end of the tailgate. "Just because I went to dinner with you last night doesn't mean I gave you a license to handle me."

Clearly amused by her outburst, he shook his head. "Oh Kerry, don't go getting all serious on me. I stole a kiss because I was glad to see you. Not because I think you're a fast and loose woman."

He made kissing her sound so simple and harmless. And maybe it was for him. But her heart was still galloping at a sickening pace and even worse, she was having to fight to stop herself from sliding back to his side.

"Okay," she conceded. "Maybe I am guilty of overreacting."

He continued to grin at her. "No. You're guilty of being too serious."

Without warning, he reached out and took a strand of her hair and rolled it between the pads of his fingers, making Kerry silently groan at the sensual contact.

"What are you doing now?" she asked.

"Looking at your hair. It's beautiful. Did you know that? It has a blue sheen to it. Like a crow."

She tried not to take his compliment to heart but it went there anyway and filled her with ridiculous pleasure.

"Crows are scavengers," she pointed out. "I'm not so sure it's a compliment to be likened to a crow."

His fingers meshed into the black silkiness until the tips were lightly touching her scalp. To Kerry the contact was almost as intimate as the kiss from his lips.

"George can tell you all sorts of stories about the crow," he said. "They're a highly intelligent and tenacious bird, two qualities admired by the Comanche."

She swallowed as the nervous beating of her heart seemed to rise up in her throat. "And it's impossible to sneak up on one," she added. "So you shouldn't try it."

Her words of warning caused him to laugh and he pulled his hand away from her.

"I'll remember that, Kerry. So tell me, what are you doing here this evening?"

Kerry dared to glance at him. The hair falling across his forehead was dark enough to be called black. Yet here in the brighter light of day, she could see threads of deep brown and russet. Like his gray eyes, the subtle shades in his hair were a throwback to his white blood, she supposed.

"Before I go into that, I'd like to know why you didn't mention anything to me about getting a key to the city?" she asked. "You must have known I would see your picture in the paper."

A sheepish expression stole over his face. "Oh. So you saw that little piece."

She nodded. "One of the loan officers at the bank showed it to me. It looked as though the mayor had quite a little ceremony for you."

"Believe me, Kerry. I didn't ask for any of that. Actually, I tried to get out of the whole thing, but Bram wouldn't let me. With him being the elected sheriff of Comanche County, it would have reflected badly on him to have his brother refuse such a nice gesture from the town leader."

He sounded apologetic, which caused Kerry's brows to lift with surprise. "There's no need to apologize, Jared. I was only wondering why you didn't mention it last night. I would have been watching for the article in the paper today. As it was, I learned about it secondhand."

Jared shrugged. "I guess I stupidly hoped you wouldn't see it." He reached for her hand and gently smoothed it between both of his. "I don't want you thinking I saved Peggy just to garner attention for myself. I might have been guilty of being a ham back in my younger days. But nowadays I'd just as soon stay in the background."

He actually seemed embarrassed by all the notoriety he'd been receiving these past few days. Which didn't fit in with her image of a playboy, at all. The notion put a soft smile on her face.

"You saved Peggy because you cared about her. Just as you would any other child. I've never believed anything else."

He released her hand and smiled at her. Not a teasing or humorous smile. But a genuine smile of gladness. "It's a relief to hear you say that, Kerry."

Oh Kerry, this man is smooth. Too smooth for you.

In spite of the inner warning, her heart melted like a gooey candy bar. "Uh—the reason I'm here is—well, it's going to sound strange. But I decided you should know about it."

He looked intrigued. "Now you've stirred my curiosity. Tell me."

Feeling a bit foolish, she shook her head. "I don't really know how to start, especially when this is hearsay. But Clarence, he's a loan officer at Liberty National—he told me that a stranger was in the courthouse yesterday looking up information on your grandmother and all her descendants. Clarence suggested that the man probably had intentions of doing a story about you. But I told him that wasn't the normal way to go about it."

Jared studied her for long moments and just about the time Kerry expected him to burst out laughing, a concerned frown marred his forehead.

"That's odd," he said. "Where did your co-worker get this story?"

"Straight from the courthouse," Kerry told him.

Thoughtfully, Jared stroked a thumb and forefinger against his chin. "And he—this stranger was looking into Gloria's history?"

"That's the story Clarence gave me."

"Hmm. Maybe he's doing a book on Comanches," Jared reasoned. "Although she married a white man, she's full Comanche and so is George."

Kerry considered his suggestion. "Could be," she agreed, "but the Comanche tribe numbers around ten thousand right now. That's not very many people compared to the rest of the population. However, it is when you consider that most of them live in or around Black Arrow. So why would your grandmother's life be singled out? Unless it has something to do with you being in the news here lately."

Jared shrugged. "I don't see any connection."

"Neither could I. That's why I thought I should tell

you about it," Kerry said, then asked, "can you think of anything connected to your grandmother that might make someone interested in her genealogy?"

His head swung back and forth. "Not really. Except for the time she spent in Nevada, she's lived right here in Black Arrow all her life. Everyone knows her and all of us Coltons."

"Maybe you Coltons have some land this person is interested in. Land that may have changed hands through the family," Kerry suggested.

He shot her a guilty look. "To be honest, Kerry, I don't keep up with all the goings on in my family. As long as I know they're healthy and happy, I don't interfere in their lives. So if this stranger did have some connection to Gloria, I doubt I'd know about it."

"Maybe you should ask her," Kerry went on.

Once again, Jared shook his head. "No. She works hard in the Feed and Grain store. And at her age, she doesn't need any more stress than that. And if you're wondering why us kids don't make her retire, well, believe me we've tried. I do know that much."

"Well, there's probably nothing to this courthouse thing anyway," she replied.

Jared said, "Just the same, I think I'll talk to Bram about it. He might know what's going on."

"That's probably a good idea," she agreed, then with a pointed glance at their entwined hands, she cleared her throat. "You'd better let me go now. I have to get back home."

"So soon? You just got here!"

"We've been sitting here longer than you think," she told him. Definitely long enough for her senses to go bounding off in all the wrong directions, she thought. "And I'm keeping you from your job."

He flashed her a crooked grin. "I'm the boss. And a good one. I don't have to ride my men with a whip. They know what I expect from them and they do it."

Yes, he was a man who knew exactly how to get what he wanted from people, Kerry silently agreed. Especially women. And if her ordeal with Damon had taught her anything, it was to never let herself be manipulated by another man. Even one as sweet and sexy as Jared Colton.

Drawing in a bracing breath, she glanced toward the direction of the WindWalker house. "Mom and Peggy went to visit a friend in Indiahoma. They might be back by now and if I'm not home, Mom will be wondering."

She glanced back at him and immediately saw the wheels turning in his gray eyes.

"I'm not about to let you go home now," he said softly.

"Jared—what are you doing? Stop!" she cried as he grabbed her around the waist and lifted her down to the ground beside him.

"Don't argue," he said, "or I'll kiss you again."

His hands were warm and possessive, while the sultry gleam in his eyes backed up his playful threat. The eager beat of her heart warned Kerry that she'd be in big trouble if he kissed her again.

"All right," she murmured submissively. "I suppose I can spare a few more minutes."

"That's better," he said smugly. "Now let me help you into the truck and I'll go tell the guys I'm leaving."

Kerry remained silent as he assisted her into his four-wheel drive truck, but once he returned from talking with his crew, she said, "Jared, I didn't come here to—to go out with you!"

He shook his head as he started the truck's engine. "We have to eat supper and since you're alone and I'm alone, we'll eat it together."

She groaned at his persistence. "I've already eaten a sandwich."

He shot her a grin as he wheeled the truck onto the nearest street. "Then we'll go have a milkshake."

Kerry very nearly laughed. "Milkshake! I thought men like you took a woman out for cocktails. Strong ones."

His low chuckles were as sensual as the glint in his gray eyes. "What do you know about men like me?"

"Mainly that you're dangerous."

The amusement on his face disappeared and before Kerry could guess his intentions, he reached for her hand and brought it to his lips.

"I would never harm a hair on your head, sweetheart."

But what about her heart? Kerry wondered. She couldn't lose it to this man who was content to live his life roving from one job to the next, from one woman to the next.

Ten minutes later the two of them were parked at a local drive-in. The truck windows were rolled down to catch the evening breeze and a few feet away, the faint sound of rock 'n' roll music was filtering out from a car radio. Young waitresses dressed in shorts and roller skates weaved their way around the parked vehicles to serve trays of drinks and fast food.

Since Kerry knew that Jared had to be hungry after a long day at work, she'd insisted he order himself a meal, while she settled for a vanilla milkshake.

Once they were served their order, Jared brought up the subject of the courthouse stranger again.

"I've been doing some thinking about the whole thing," he said, "And I've decided you and I should take a look at those records in the courthouse. Maybe we could figure out what the man was really looking for. Because I tell you one thing, Kerry, the more I study about it, the more I'm convinced he wasn't just a genealogy buff."

Kerry stared at him as two words stuck in her mind. "You and I? We should go over the records? What about Bram? Shouldn't he be the one looking into this matter?"

Jared swallowed down a mouthful of French fry before he shook his head. "My brother is already bogged down with paperwork, much less all the emergency calls he has to respond to. Besides, I think we need to be a little sneaky about this. Otherwise, we might alert this person that we're on to him. If Bram suddenly showed up at the courthouse asking questions, the whole story would spread like wildfire."

She squared around in the seat so that she was facing him. "You're probably right about that, Jared. But when would you and I have a chance to go over records in the courthouse? We both have jobs. And I can't afford to miss work."

"And I wouldn't ask you to," he assured her. "We'll go after work."

Her mouth fell open. "Jared, what are you thinking? The courthouse closes at five, the same time we bank workers leave the building. We couldn't get in."

His expression said he wasn't the least bit deterred by that minor problem. "Hey, I got a key to the city, didn't I? Surely I can get us into the courthouse after working hours.''

Maybe he could, Kerry thought. But spending time alone with Jared would be asking for big trouble. He was already kissing her, touching her as though he had the right. As though he was certain she wanted to be connected to him in that way. How would she be able to resist the man? Darn it all, she couldn't!

''You really don't need me tagging along with you, Jared. This is about your family. You would know much more about what to look for than I would.''

His sly grin said he wasn't about to let her wiggle out of the task. ''Maybe. But two heads are much better than one. And you are the one who so sweetly informed me about this stranger in the first place,'' he reminded her.

He was right, she silently admitted. She was the one who'd brought this whole matter up to him. If she'd cared enough to tell him about the stranger, she ought to be willing to help him do a little investigative work.

''All right. I'll help,'' she agreed. ''When did you want to start?''

''I've got a meeting with the representative of a drilling company later tonight. And I'll need time to get a key to the building,'' he said thoughtfully. ''What about tomorrow night at seven? I'll pick you up.''

''No!'' she blurted out loudly, then quickly added, ''I mean, I'll meet you there.''

The close scrutiny of his gray eyes turned her cheeks a deep, rosy shade. ''What's the matter? Afraid your mother will meet me at the door with a shotgun?''

Maybe he thought it was funny, but Enola's attitude was like a worrisome splinter in her foot. Glancing away from him, she said, "My mother doesn't like you."

Jared was more amused than offended by Kerry's admission. Chuckling softly, he said, "Kerry, you're a grown woman. Isn't it about time you picked your own friends?"

Did he think of himself as her friend? she wondered. He seemed like so much more to her. Which only proved that she was getting in way too deep for her own good.

"Enola doesn't run my life. I'm just—oh, she thinks you're a sorry, no-account womanizer."

The amusement on his face rapidly disappeared. "And what do you think I am?" he asked gently.

A good man, she thought. A man that cared about his family and friends, and the men who worked for him. He was also a man who was capable of breaking her heart. If she was crazy enough to give him the chance.

"I don't—necessarily think you're a womanizer," she said. "You're just a man who likes women. And that's not a crime. Nor does it stop us from being friends."

His gray eyes turned rueful as he reached over and stroked a finger down her bare arm. "I guess I'll never be able to live down my past entirely," he said. "But for what it's worth, Kerry, I don't have a bunch of women in my life. In fact, you're the first woman I've kissed in...let's just say a long time."

Kerry desperately wanted to believe him. She wanted to think she was special to this man. But she wasn't totally naive. Sooner or later Jared would be leaving Black Arrow and when he did, she would be nothing more to him than a pleasant memory.

"I doubt you could convince Enola of that," she said, deliberately trying to keep her tone light and teasing. "But if you insist on picking me up at the house—then okay, I'll be ready at seven."

"Good," he said with a pleased grin. "Maybe the two of us can put our heads together and figure out what's so interesting about my grandmother's family tree."

Chapter Eight

The next evening Jared left the excavation site early to drop by the sheriff's office. Bram was in the parking lot about to climb into his truck when Jared trotted up to him.

"What's the hurry?" Bram asked. "Is there a problem out at the site?"

"No. I need to talk to you about something. I tried to call you last night, but you wouldn't answer the phone."

"I had a meeting with the civil defense. It didn't end until late," he explained. "Why didn't you leave a message?"

Jared leaned a shoulder against the door of Bram's truck. "Because I wanted to talk directly to you about this."

One of Bram's brows lifted with amused intrigue. "What's this about? Kerry WindWalker?"

Jared scowled at him. Joking about his female conquests in the past was one thing, but clumping Kerry in that same group bothered the hell out of him.

"No. I don't need advice on my love life or lack of it," he said in a voice gruff enough to cause Bram's eyes to widen. "This is about our grandmother and our family. Somebody is trying to stick their nose into our personal business."

Bram's expression turned serious. "What are you talking about? Has someone been harassing Grandmother at the feed store?"

Jared shook his head. "Apparently you haven't heard. A man was at the courthouse a couple of days ago asking to see records on Gloria Colton and her descendants."

"Who was it? I'll have him checked out."

"Not that simple, brother. Apparently the man was a stranger."

Bram absently scratched his cheek. "Hmm, that's odd. I wonder why he didn't question Grandmother or me?"

"That's what Kerry and I wondered, too."

Bram looked at him. "Kerry? I thought this wasn't about her?"

"It isn't. I mean, it isn't directly about her. She's the one who told me about the stranger. She was worried that he might be up to some mischief toward our family."

Grinning now, Bram said, "Sounds like you've already gotten her in the palm of your hand."

"Damn it, Bram. I'm not trying to get Kerry—" he stopped abruptly as he realized he was unwilling and even uncertain as to how to go on. On one hand he wasn't trying to "get" Kerry in the way that Bram was thinking. But then he had to admit that he was more than mildly interested in the woman. All his waking thoughts were centered around her and spending every available moment he could with her was becoming a craving he couldn't seem to assuage or dismiss. Still, he wasn't about to admit he was falling in love. That was something that Jared Colton just didn't do. "And you quit trying to change the subject."

"All right," Bram relented, "back to this stranger. You don't have a name or description of the man?"

Jared shook his head. "No. But in the meantime, I'd like to have a key to the courthouse so that Kerry and I can search through the family records and see if we can come up with a reason for somebody to be snooping."

Bram let out one mocking laugh. "You want a key to the courthouse. Just like that. Well, so would a lot of other people, little brother. It's always an advantage to know whose property is coming up at the next sheriff's sale."

"Hell, Bram. I'm not hunting land that's about to go for unpaid taxes! I only want to look at the birth, marriage and death records. They might tell us something."

Bram laid an assuring hand on his brother's shoulder. "Look Jared, I think you're blowing this whole thing out of proportion. Everyone knows us Coltons. We don't have any skeletons in the closet. Forget about it and let the stranger look all he wants."

Jared sighed. "Bram, you wanted me to humor you about that damn key to the city thing. Now it's your turn to indulge me about this. 'Cause frankly, I think something fishy is going on and I want to know what it is."

Bram held up one hand before Jared could further argue his case. "All right. I'll see what I can do. Come back by the office in about an hour and I'll have a key rounded up for you. But you'd better make sure you guard the thing with your life. And I'd better not hear of anything left out of place."

Jared affectionately slapped a hand on his brother's arm. "Thanks Bram. And don't worry. No one will ever know we've been anywhere near the courthouse. Much less inside it."

The Comanche County courthouse was situated on a city block that also included the Liberty National Bank building. Most days Kerry gave the government building little more than a passing glance. And never in her wildest dreams did she think she and Jared Colton would be sneaking into the back door, long after closing hours. She still wasn't sure why she was there at all. Except that once he'd invited her to join him, she'd not been able to turn down the chance to spend this quiet time with him.

"Do you know where the records are kept?" Kerry whispered to Jared as the two of them headed down a wide, dimly lit corridor.

Grinning, he reached for her hand. "You don't have to whisper, Kerry. I don't think anyone on the outside can hear us. And I sure as heck don't expect anyone in this place to be working after hours."

The feel of his fingers twined around hers was uniquely intimate and as they walked forward into the dark cavernous building it was easy for Kerry to imagine that Jared was leading her to his own private lair instead of a room with a bunch of file cabinets filled with old documents.

"Okay," she said in a more normal tone of voice. "Do you know where you're taking us?"

"Let's look for a sign. Maybe we'll get lucky and the door will be labeled."

Jared's assumption turned out to be correct. In one corner on the bottom floor, they found a door labeled Records. Once inside, Jared shut the blinds on the window, then switched on the overhead light. After that, it was easy to find the alphabetically filed documents.

The two of them pulled out everything they could find on Gloria and her twin sons Trevor and Thomas, then carried it all over to a small table equipped with padded metal chairs.

"What about the grandchildren?" Kerry asked as they sat shoulder to shoulder. "There's what? Ten or eleven of you?"

"Eleven. So we can't possibly go through each one of them tonight. We'll have to come back tomorrow night."

She arched her brows at him. "You expect me to come back here tomorrow night? With you?"

He chuckled at her dismay. "You make it sound as though I've brought you to a house of sin instead of a stuffy old courthouse."

One of her shoulders lifted and fell. "That's exactly what my mother thinks."

He laughed with ease, then sobered as he watched a scowl wrinkle her face. "Still giving you problems over me?"

"She's moved on to the silent treatment now. So I don't want to imagine her reaction if I asked her to watch Peggy again tomorrow night. While I go out again with you."

"Well, I wouldn't mind if you brought Peggy with us," he suggested.

Kerry glanced around the shadowy room lined with rows of tall metal file cabinets. It was hardly the place to keep a child quietly occupied.

"It's sweet of you to offer, Jared," she said, "but Peggy would be whining in no time flat. Especially if she couldn't have Claws with her."

Resting his arm along the back of her chair, he eased closer until his chest was very nearly touching her arm. "Don't make the mistake of thinking I'm sweet, Kerry. I'm not. I'm selfish. Most men are, you know. And even if I wasn't concerned about some stranger digging into my family's private business, I'd still be searching for a way to spend time with you."

His frankness shouldn't have surprised her. After all, he'd made it pretty clear that he was physically attracted to her. But hearing him say it like this with the two of them so totally secluded, set her heart to pounding and her mind to wondering. Just how far did he intend to take this allure he had for her? As far as she would let him?

Licking her lips, she reached for the documents lying on the table in front of them. "I think—we'd better get to work. Before someone comes in here and catches us."

He chuckled softly and the sensual sound slithered down Kerry's spine. More and more she wanted to touch this man, to feel the excitement of his arms around her. And most of all, to taste his lips. Little by little, he was seducing her and he wasn't even trying.

"This stuff we have here is public records," Jared rationalized. "Anyone can look at it. All they have to do is ask."

"Yes, but do we have a right to be in here after hours? I'm sure Bram has stuck his neck out by giving you that key."

Shrugging, he said, "Bram has important friends in this town. And he knows he can trust me."

She waggled a handful of papers at him. "Then we'd better get to work."

With a good-natured groan, he eased back from her. "All right. You win. For now," he added with a promising wink.

More than an hour and a half later, Jared leaned back in his chair and released a frustrated sigh. "I don't know about you, Kerry, but this stuff we've been studying is boring to me. There's nothing unusual here. It's all birth certificates and my parents' death certificates. And so far all the names and dates look correct to me. I don't understand why anyone would need this sort of information."

Kerry thoughtfully glanced at the papers still scattered on the tabletop. She and Jared had pored over the documents and so far none of the information had come as a surprise to Jared. As he'd said before, his relatives were all natives of Black Arrow. The information was mundane.

Yes, to him, she thought suddenly. But not to a stranger.

"Jared," she said mindfully. "Maybe we're not seeing anything here because we already know this information. But obviously the stranger didn't. Something about these dates or names might be important to him."

A quizzical frown wrinkled his dark features. "But why?"

Kerry had been trying to think of all the possibilities, but so far all of them seemed lame.

She glanced at him as another thought struck her. "Are you sure someone in your family hasn't hired someone to do a family tree?"

Jared tossed the paper he was holding onto the table with the rest. "I don't know why. Gloria has a bible with everyone's name and birthday written in it. Anyone could get all this information from her."

Kerry carefully considered his remark. "Which makes me believe this man doesn't want to have contact with the Colton family. Nor does he want you to know he's been prying into your background."

Jared slowly nodded in agreement. "I think you're right. But Bram wasn't very alarmed when I told him about the stranger. He thinks the whole thing is probably harmless."

"Well, everything we've come up with so far is speculative," Kerry had to agree.

"True," Jared admitted, "but it's still weird. And I'm not going to rest until I find out just what the jerk is up to."

Kerry folded her arms across her breasts as she studied him with new regard. "You know, this mission seems out of character for you."

A wry grin twisted his lips. "Why is that? I'm not the James Bond type?"

She shook her head. "No. You're not the family type. And you told me earlier that you've always been guilty of not keeping up with family interests. Why the concern now?"

Her question was something Jared had been asking himself. Bram probably suspected that he was doing this little investigation only as a means to spend time with Kerry. And that might be partially true. But it wasn't the main reason he felt driven to protect the family. Something had happened to him that night he'd pulled Peggy from the dark, suffocating pipe and placed her in Kerry's arms.

Seeing the terror in Kerry's eyes change to joyous relief had jolted him from the happy-go-lucky life he'd tried to lead since he'd lost his parents. Taking life lightly had become second nature to him. If he always laughed, he reasoned with himself, there'd never be room for tears. But experiencing firsthand the close call with Peggy had made him see even more just how fleeting and precious life could be.

A sheepish smile touched his lips. "You've been telling me how lucky I am to belong to a big loving family," he said, "and I guess it's dawned on me that you're right. I'm fortunate to have them all and if I can help to keep them safe and happy, then that's what I want to do."

The corners of her lips curled upward into a tempting grin. "You'd better be careful, Jared Colton, or you're going to lose your reputation as a playboy."

Chuckling, he started gathering the documents together. "Come on," he told her. "Let's put these things back where they belong and get out of here. We'll look the others over tomorrow night."

Carefully, the two of them returned the records to the correct slots in the file cabinets, then turned off the light and reopened the blinds.

At the back exit, Jared let the two of them out into the warm night. While he locked the door, Kerry stood close beside him and surveyed the shadowy clumps of shrubs that randomly dotted the lawn.

As her eyes reached the far corner of the building,

she saw the limbs on one of shrubs rustle, then grow still. There was no wind tonight and the only sound she could hear was that of the light traffic traveling the main street in front of the building, yet she was quite certain someone was near.

"Hurry up with that lock, Jared," she whispered softly. "I think someone is watching us."

Jared pulled the key from the slot and rattled the door to make sure it was solidly locked before he turned around and took her by the upper arm. "Did you see someone? Where?"

"At the end of the building there." She pointed directly in front of them to a spot where the building jutted up to a low stone wall. "That shrub was moving. And it couldn't have been the wind. We don't have any tonight."

Instead of laughing away her suggestion, he lifted his head and studied the whole area around them. About thirty feet away, a graveled parking area was dimly lit with two streetlights. At the moment, the only vehicle in sight was Jared's white truck. Between it and the spot where they stood was a wide lawn shaded by a huge sycamore tree and dotted randomly with several head-high shrubs. If someone was lurking nearby, it would be easy to keep to the shadows and go unnoticed. But why would someone be lingering about the courthouse at this time of night, he wondered. No one but Bram had been aware that Jared was going to be here. Unless someone had been following him, he thought grimly.

"Wait here and I'll go look," he said, keeping his voice low.

"No!" Kerry cried. "You're not leaving me alone back here! I'll go with you."

Recognizing fear in her voice, he took her hand and squeezed it. "All right," he conceded, "but stay behind me. And don't say a word."

Slowly they crept to the corner of the building where Kerry had seen the movement. By the time they reached the dense darkness created by the bush, her heart was pounding with fear and she wondered what she would do if someone stepped out of the shadows and attacked them. No doubt Jared was man enough to handle himself. But not if he was distracted with trying to save her.

She gripped his hand tightly as he edged toward the corner of the building, then peered furtively around the huge, hand-hewn sandstone.

"There's no one here now," he whispered. "Let's get out of here."

He kept Kerry close to his side until they reached the truck, then quickly he unlocked the vehicle and helped her inside. Once he was behind the wheel, he touched the electronic button to lock the doors.

"You really think someone might have been hiding in the shadows?" Kerry asked him. "I expected you to laugh at me for suggesting such a thing."

He gave the secluded area around them another long search before he started the truck and pulled out of the parking lot.

"We may both be crazy," Jared told her as he maneuvered the truck onto a nearby street. "But something back there was making the hair on the back of my neck stand on end."

Kerry outwardly shivered. "Jared, this—whatever it

is—is not some harmless genealogy buff digging up records.''

"No," he agreed. "That's why we have to find what this man is looking for before he has the chance to find it himself.''

The next evening, instead of asking her mother to baby-sit for her while she helped Jared at the courthouse, she drove Peggy over to stay with her friend, Christa.

"Don't worry about the two of us," Christa told Kerry as the two women stood in the living room of Christa's apartment. "We're going to have great fun with some new acrylic paints I just bought.''

Before her marriage had crumbled, Christa had longed to have a baby of her own. Since that wish hadn't materialized, the other woman always jumped at the chance to spend time with Peggy. And thankfully, Peggy was already ready to visit her "aunt" Christa.

Kerry groaned good-naturedly. "It's a good thing I let her wear an old T-shirt and shorts. Just don't let her smear the stuff in her hair. It's just now growing out from the wad of bubble gum I had to cut from the back.''

Christa laughed. "I'll tie a kerchief around her head.''

Glancing at her watch, Kerry said, "I'll be back to pick her up by nine.''

"Like I said, we'll be fine," Christa assured her as she followed her friend to the door.

"Thanks, Christa, you've saved me from having another round with my mother."

The young blonde shook her head with disapproval. "Kerry, I understand it's financially better for you to live with your mother. But, believe me, money isn't everything. I let Steven get away with thousands just to get rid of him. Your mother has no right to dictate who you see or where you go."

With a weary sigh, Kerry pushed a hand through her thick black hair. "I know, Christa. And one day soon I'm going to start making plans to move. But right now—well, Mother loves us. And we're all she really has. She's giving me problems about Jared because she's afraid I'm going to get hurt."

Christa's expression became knowing as she studied Kerry's troubled face. "You are getting serious about the man, aren't you?"

Kerry opened her mouth to protest, but instead her shoulders slumped with defeat and she lowered her voice so it wouldn't reach Peggy, who was sitting on the floor in front of Christa's television.

"I don't know, Christa. I keep telling myself that the man is just a friend, but when I'm with him, I feel...more alive than I have in a long, long time."

Christa grinned and waggled her eyebrows. "I can see why. The man looks as sexy as sin."

"He is as sexy as sin. And Mom is probably right. I shouldn't be spending time with him. But..."

"But you want to," Christa finished with a wicked wink.

Nodding, Kerry let out a rueful sigh. "Do you think I'm crazy?"

Christa's playful grin suddenly sobered. "Look Kerry, as men go, we've both had a couple of losers in our lives. But I'll be darned if I let Steven ruin the rest of my life. And you shouldn't let Damon ruin yours. You need to get out and enjoy yourself. And as far as I can see, there's nothing wrong with enjoying yourself with Jared."

Kerry glanced at Peggy to make sure she wasn't picking up any of the conversation. It would be highly embarrassing if her daughter started repeating things to Jared.

"Christa, the man is—or at least he was, a lady's man. He probably changes his women each time he finishes a job. I can't expect any more from him."

Christa looked at her closely. "Do you want more from him?"

She did, damn it. Somehow, the man had worked his way under her skin. She was to the point where she needed to be with him. Just having him near, listening to his voice, seeing him smile, filled her whole being with joy. Now that he'd come into her life, she couldn't imagine giving him up.

"I'm afraid I do, Christa," she whispered miserably. "And I know that's crazy. Because I know Jared Colton. I've known him since I was a small girl. He used to be one of those reckless bad boys. You know, the kind that wore his hair just a tad too long and roared around the streets on a Harley."

"And the girls all swooned at his feet," Christa added.

Kerry nodded glumly. "And now I'm swooning when I should be running."

"Oh Kerry, you're thinking about this in the wrong way. Jared is older now. He's probably a changed man. And for all you know, he might be getting serious about you."

Kerry was suddenly remembering the embrace they'd shared on George WhiteBear's porch. For the most part his kiss had been exciting and sexy. Yet underneath those things, she'd felt a tender desire that had caught her off guard and had almost made her believe he might care about her. Almost, but not quite.

"Jared serious about me?" Her light laughter had nothing to do with being amused. "No, Christa. Jared is a man who likes to enjoy himself. And he likes female company. That's all there is to it. And I'm not about to make the mistake of thinking otherwise."

Christa shook her head. "Kerry—"

"I've got to go, Christa. Jared is probably waiting for me. I'll see you about nine."

Before the other woman could say more, Kerry quickly blew a goodbye kiss to her daughter, then let herself out of the apartment.

By the time Kerry parked next to Jared's truck in the courthouse parking lot, he was waiting at her car door to greet her.

The sight of his tall, muscular body dressed in jeans and a pale blue polo shirt stirred her senses, but it was the warm smile on his face that touched her heart and made her very, very glad to see him.

"Six minutes late. I was beginning to think I was being stood up," he said as she climbed out on the ground beside him.

"Sorry. It took a few minutes to get away from

Christa's," she explained, wondering what he would think if she told him that she and Christa had been discussing him. Probably give her a smug laugh, she thought.

"You're forgiven," he said softly, then taking her by the shoulders he drew her into his arms.

Kerry didn't question or protest his actions. Instead, her heart drummed with eager anticipation as she lifted her face up to his.

"Aren't we supposed to be heading into the building?" she asked huskily.

He lowered his head to hers. "First things first," he whispered against her lips.

Kerry was helpless to resist the desire to taste his lips, to feel the warmth of his body firing hers. Mindlessly, she closed her eyes and lifted her arms to circle his neck. While his lips made a hungry foray of hers, she felt his hands roaming her back, her rib cage, then lower to where her waist curved to the top of her hips.

Heat and need rushed through her like a bolt of lightning, making her cling to him like a wet, shivering puppy. She would have been happy to stand there kissing him forever, but after a few minutes he broke the contact of their lips and rested his forehead against hers.

"I think we'd better go in before I forget why we're here," he murmured.

He was right about that, she thought. One more minute and she wouldn't have cared if they'd been standing in the middle of main street, just as long as he kept on making love to her.

She drew in a ragged breath. "Uh—just a minute. I'd like to know what that little kiss was for?"

His sexy grin flashed at her through the semidarkness. "I wasn't aware that was a little kiss. You must be a hard woman to please. But believe me, it will be a joy trying."

She groaned at his nonsense and the desire still churning in the pit of her stomach. "That's not what I meant. Why tonight? Now?"

The grin of pleasure remained on his face. "When I drove you home last night, you jumped out of the truck so fast, I didn't have the chance to get a hand on you. So I was making up for the loss now."

Kerry had made a quick exit last night. Mainly because she'd been afraid. Their private time together in the courthouse had heightened her senses and made her desperately aware of how much she wanted to get close to him. If she'd allowed him to kiss her, she might not have been able to stop herself from begging him for more. Even now she wanted to tell him to forget about the dusty documents inside the courthouse and take her to some hidden place where there was nothing but the two of them.

Oh my, she was losing it, she thought desperately. She had to shake away this sensual spell he'd put over her, before she wound up being one more notch on the headboard of Jared Colton's bed.

"I see," she said in a voice that still sounded breathless to her own ears. "And what makes you think you're supposed to get a hand on me?"

Chuckling, he curled one arm around her shoulders and began to guide her toward the back entrance of the building. "Great-grandfather George said the Great Spirit had made you for me. I can't argue with that kind of reasoning."

"You told me that you Colton children don't believe half of what George says. Why should you put any stock in that one prophetic statement?"

His hand tightened on her shoulder. "Because this time I happen to agree with him."

Kerry was so stunned by his comment she couldn't utter a word. But once she did collect herself, she decided the best thing she could do was let the whole thing slide.

He probably sweet-talked every woman he'd ever wooed, she told herself. And as for George White-Bear's prediction, Jared probably considered the whole thing as nothing more than amusing words from an old, old man.

Chapter Nine

Inside the building, Kerry and Jared walked straight to the records room. After Jared had shut the blinds and turned on the light, the two of them went to the file cabinets and pulled all the documents they hadn't had time to examine the night before.

Once they'd taken seats at the table, Kerry asked, "Did you tell Bram that we thought someone was watching us last night?"

"No. I tried to call him today while I was at work, but he was out of the office. I'll catch him later. And maybe by then we'll have something more concrete to tell him." He glanced at her. "What did you tell your mother you were doing tonight?"

Kerry's gaze skittered away from his. "I told her the truth. That I was helping you with a family matter. She thinks I'm headed for a heartache by keeping company with you."

As soon as the words were out, Kerry bit down on her lip. She didn't know what had made her say such a thing to him. After their little interlude in the parking lot, she'd intended to keep their conversation off the personal.

"And what do you think?" he asked solemnly.

"That I'm headed for a heartache," she whispered hoarsely.

"Oh Kerry." With a shake of his head, he reached for her hand and threaded his fingers through hers. "I don't know why you think I'm some evil snake out to bite you at any moment. I told you last night I wouldn't harm a hair on your head."

The gentleness in his voice only made her throat tighten that much more. If this man loved her and left her as Damon had, she didn't think she could live through it. Not a second time.

"Not intentionally."

"Not in any way."

Her gaze dropped to the table top. "I'm not looking for fun and games, Jared. I'm not like you."

His brows inched upward over his gray eyes. "What makes you think I'm looking for fun and games?"

One of her shoulders lifted and fell. She didn't want to have this conversation with him. She'd only wind up humiliating herself and making him feel awkward.

"As far as I know you've always lived that way."

His lips compressed to a thin line. "And you expect me to do what I've always done for the rest of my life? Did you ever think I might be ready for a change?"

She couldn't stop the faint flutter of hope in her heart. Lifting wide eyes to his, she said, "You're still young, Jared. Being tied down with a family is not what you want."

"So you're telling me that you know more about what I want, than I do myself."

He sounded irritated with her, but Kerry couldn't help it. She had to be honest. She had to make it clear that she wasn't in the market for an affair with him. No matter how sweet and wonderful it might be.

Her head bobbed up and down. "I'm not that same naive young woman who used to waitress at Woody's Café. I've learned not to believe everything a man says."

Jared's nostrils flared with disgust as he studied her face. "Look Kerry, I'm not like Peggy's father. If I had a child somewhere, she wouldn't have to wonder where her father was or why he didn't want her."

His bluntness reddened her cheeks. "I didn't say you were like him. I meant—oh, I don't want to talk about this, Jared. It's…pointless."

Tearing her hand from his, she quickly jumped to her feet and walked over to stand in front of the room's sole window. She was staring unseeingly at the closed blinds when she felt him move up behind her. His sigh was audible as he placed both his hands on the backs of her shoulders.

"Kerry, I don't know what you want me to say," he said quietly. "I don't know what you want from me."

Her eyes closed, she tried to swallow away the lump of tangled emotions in her throat. "Honesty, Jared. That's what I really want." She turned suddenly to face him, her eyes challenging him to open up to her. "So don't tell me you're looking at me with marriage on your mind. I won't believe you."

His hands gently cupped the sides of her face. And

in spite of her doubts about his feelings, his touch made her heart beat with excitement and joy.

"Kerry, I'll try to be as honest with you as I can be. But that's hard to do when…I'm not sure—" He broke off with a shake of his head. "When I first saw you running up to me that evening when Peggy was lost, I was—well, shaken. Don't ask me why. Because I can't explain it. I only know I was very, very glad to see you and to learn that you were back in Black Arrow." He grinned wryly as he added, "Don't you remember me asking you for a date? Way back, after you just graduated high school?"

If her face had been red before, she knew it was absolutely burning with color now. No doubt his hands could feel the heat traveling up her neck and into her cheeks.

"Yes. I remember. But you dated many girls back then. I didn't want to be just another number."

As Jared's gaze slipped over her face, then settled on her chocolate brown eyes, he realized she'd never been just another girl to him. Nor could she ever be. Besides her dark beauty, there was something about her, a quiet, graceful dignity that pulled at him, that told him if she ever loved a man, it would be with a deep forever kind of passion.

"I thought you didn't like me," he said.

She couldn't stop the faint smile that spread across her face. "I liked you. But I was very scared of you."

His brows lifted in question at the same time his hands decided to dig into her silky hair and push it back from her oval face. "Scared?"

She nodded. "You were way too old and too sexy for me."

He chuckled softly. "Too old? I don't like the sound of that. But the too sexy is flattering."

The nearness of his body tempted her to step forward and slide her arms around his waist, to bury her face against his chest and simply stand there until she'd drunk her fill of his male scent and the strong security of his body.

"So you're telling me you wanted to go out with me now, because I refused to date you back then."

His grin turned sheepish as he continued to play with her hair. "Something like that. You sorta squashed my pride back then. I thought catching your attention now would make up for your rejection." His expression sobered as he brushed his fingertips against her cheek. "But I wasn't counting on—liking you this much, Kerry."

Liking. To Kerry that was almost as important as loving and the idea that Jared might care that much for her, shook her through and through.

"Jared—"

"I know," he gently interrupted. "You don't put much stock in what I say. But you will. Sooner or later, I'll make you believe in me."

He was tempting her to peek down a primrose path, to believe that something special could happen between them. Kerry desperately wanted to imagine the two of them together. Not for just a few days or months, but forever. Yet at this moment, all she could envision was losing her heart to him, then watching him wave goodbye.

"Maybe," she murmured, then with a great breath, she ducked away from him and hurried toward the door. "I'm going to the rest room. I'll be back in a few minutes," she tossed over her shoulder.

In the shadowy hallway outside the door, Kerry walked until she found a ladies' rest room. She didn't really need to use the facilities, but she needed time to collect herself and try to remember what she was actually supposed to be doing here tonight. And it certainly wasn't falling in love with Jared!

After about six or seven minutes, Kerry decided enough time had passed for Jared to have gotten his mind off charming her and back onto the Colton family documents. She left the small cubicle and headed back to the records room.

Somewhere along the hallway, the faintest scent of smoke caught her attention, making her pause long enough to glance over her shoulder and sniff.

That wasn't someone's cigarette smoke filtering in from outside, she thought. It smelled like burning wood. Maybe someone in town had broken the rules and was burning a pile of brush in their yard, she thought.

Deciding it was nothing, Kerry headed on down the hall, but ten steps later a strange crackling noise caused her to stop dead in her tracks.

Quickly, she attempted to follow the sound and eventually found herself in front of a door marked County Tax Assessor. She twisted the knob. Locked! But the panel of wood felt warm to her hand and the hissing, sizzling sounds beyond it had to be fire!

Adrenaline shoved her into overdrive and she raced the remaining distance to the records room. "Jared! Hurry," she called to him from the doorway. "I think there's a fire in the building!"

Jumping up from his seat at the table, he hurried over to her. "Fire? What are you talking about?"

Grabbing his arm, she tugged him out in the hallway.

"In the room next to this one—at the Tax Assessor's office! I smell smoke and the door feels hot!"

After inspecting the door, Jared took only a moment to come to the same conclusion as Kerry. "Hurry. Go call 9-1-1," he instructed. "And I'll try to get the door open."

"But aren't you supposed to leave hot doors shut?" she questioned fearfully.

He nudged her toward the shaft of light spilling out into the hallway from the records room. "Don't worry about me. Just go make the call before this whole place goes up in flames!"

Not wanting to waste any more time arguing, Kerry raced to find a phone. As soon as she placed the call and repeated the necessary information to the emergency dispatcher, she ran on shaky legs back to the spot in the hallway where she'd left Jared.

The door to the burning room was now open and Jared was nowhere in sight. Apparently, he'd kicked it down and gone inside!

"Jared! Jared!"

He didn't answer and fear clawed through her like a fierce animal. She had no other choice but to follow him into the fire. If he needed help, she had to be there for him.

Stepping into the smoky room, Kerry immediately gasped at the sight. Orange flames were crawling hungrily up two entire walls and had already invaded part of the ceiling. Apparently, Jared had found a fire extinguisher from somewhere in the building and was now spraying part of the flames he could reach with the thick white foam.

Kerry hurried to his side and shouted over the din of the roaring fire. "What can I do?"

He jerked his head in the direction of her voice. "Kerry! Get out of here!"

"No! Not unless you come with me," she yelled back at him, then coughed as the dense smoke began to choke her. "The ceiling is already on fire! It might start crashing down any minute!"

By now he'd emptied the extinguisher and the flames were no more contained than when he'd first started. Tossing down the empty cylinder, he reached for her arm and began to lead her toward the door. "If the fire department doesn't get here soon, all these files and records are going to go up in flames!"

"There's nothing we can do to save it now. What about the room connecting to this one?" she asked.

He slammed the door shut on the smoke and flames, then turned to her. "I don't know. Let's see if we can find another extinguisher before the flames spread to it."

Kerry nodded. "I'll go this way," she said pointing to the nearest annex.

Before she could dash off, Jared grabbed her arm. "No. We're not going to separate now. We may have to get out of here fast and when that time comes I want to know where you are. We'll go look for an extinguisher together."

Relieved that he wasn't going to get out of her sight, Kerry bobbed her head in agreement and hand in hand they ran down the shadowy corridor, while behind them the fire burst through the door and licked at the rubbery tile covering the floor.

The eerie sound jerked Kerry's head around and she couldn't hold back a scream. "Jared! It's spreading across the hallway!"

He continued to tug her along behind him. "Don't

look back right now. Here's a fire hose. Help me get it out of the wall.''

Even though they were both working at a frantic pace, it seemed to Kerry that it took the two of them forever to get the glass door open and pull out the canvas hose. But in actuality only two or three minutes had passed by the time they got the equipment pulled down the corridor and a stream of water flowing onto the flames.

Gray smoke had begun to filter down the darkened corridor, making it difficult to breathe. Kerry wasn't sure if the sweat pouring down her face was from fear or simply caused by the skyrocketing heat of the spreading flames.

Standing close behind Jared, she watched as he aimed the blast of water on the fresh flames crawling along the floor to the records room where the two of them had been working.

''Where is the fire department?''

Kerry's frantic question was answered by a loud crash that reverberated the floor beneath their feet and had them both glancing anxiously upward.

''The ceiling in the next room has crashed in!'' Jared shouted. ''I think we'd better get out of here.''

He was about to toss down the hose and reach for Kerry when loud voices could be heard approaching from a nearby annex. Both Jared and Kerry whirled around to see a group of firefighters descending on them with hoses, axes, and other fire-fighting equipment.

''We'll take over now,'' the one who appeared to be in charge said to Jared, ''you two go on outside where it's safe.''

Wanting to get Kerry to safety, Jared grabbed her

arm and ushered her away from the flames and out the back entrance.

As they stepped out into the warm night, Kerry wailed, "Oh Jared, we left your family's documents out on the table! If that room doesn't burn, they'll know we were going through records."

"It'll be a miracle if the room doesn't burn. And anyway, I doubt that will interest the firefighters right at this moment. Look," he urged, pointing toward the roof of the building. "The flames have eaten through the roof."

The ominous sight had Kerry instinctively reaching for Jared's arm. Her fingers tightened against his flesh as she cuddled as close to him as she could get. "Jared, it's terrifying to think we might not have found the fire until we were boxed in. What do you think caused it?"

Jared had already taken his gaze off the burning roof and was now searching the grounds around them. Unlike last night, the area was now jammed with fire and rescue vehicles. Orbs of emergency lights were flashing, illuminating the firemen who were hooking up hoses and hurrying to tug them inside the building.

"The electrical wiring probably."

Something in his voice brought Kerry's gaze around to his stern profile. "You don't really think that, do you? You think—" she stopped and swallowed as the fearful image washed over her. "Someone set the fire on purpose!"

"Sssh," he said under his breath. "Don't let anyone hear you say that. At least not until Bram gets here."

Kerry's eyes widened with another horrifying thought. "Jared! You don't—we aren't going to be suspects! Dear Lord, we could have been killed!"

In an effort to soothe her, Jared pulled her into his

arms and stroked the back of her head. "I'm sorry I scared you, sweetheart. Don't worry. It's going to be all right. We'll find out what really happened."

She lifted her head from his chest to gaze up at him. "Jared, when I first told you about the stranger here at the courthouse, I didn't know it was going to cause all of this trouble. I shouldn't have said anything," she said miserably.

He continued to stroke her hair and the slender slope of her shoulders while thinking he'd never known a woman like this, one who considered others before herself. Except for his mother. And she'd been taken from him so long ago.

The thought caused him to tighten his hold and pull her even deeper into the circle of his arms. "Don't say that, Kerry. You didn't cause any of this to happen. I'm glad you did tell me. If you hadn't we might not have known something sinister was among us."

Shivering at his suggestion, Kerry clung to the hard muscles of his chest. "But to burn us—"

"We don't know if the fire was meant to hurt us, Kerry. It could have been to cover up or destroy those records we were going through."

Among the chaotic noise of idling pumper trucks and shouts of nearby firemen, Jared sensed someone had approached him from behind. With Kerry still tucked safely in the circle of his arm, he turned to see his brother Bram and from his grim expression he wasn't the least bit happy to find his town in turmoil.

"Jared, are you two okay?"

The question prompted Jared to look down at Kerry. The two of them were both marked from head to toe with dirt and black soot, along with having their clothes soaked from wrestling the fire hose down the corridor.

And they were both still dazed and shaken. But as he gently cupped his hand around her face, he realized the only thing that mattered was having Kerry safe and by his side.

"Yeah. We're both fine. Just a little wet. And shook up."

Bram lifted his hat from his head and ran a hand through his hair. "Well, thank God for that. But I'd like to know what in hell is going on, Jared? I was worried about you leaving stray papers laying around. I never dreamed you two would set the damn building on fire!"

Jared threw his palm up. "Whoa now, Bram. We didn't have anything to do with the fire. If Kerry hadn't walked down to the rest room, we might have been burning ourselves!"

Bram directed his gaze on Kerry. "What did you see?"

Kerry wiped at the wet, tangled hair falling into her face. "Actually, I didn't see anything. I walked to the rest room and was there for only a few minutes. Then on my way back to the records room, I smelled smoke and heard a strange crackling noise, like logs burning in a fireplace. So I ran to get Jared. He knocked down the door to the tax assessor records."

Bram turned his attention back to Jared. "I take it the fire was already out of control by then?"

Jared nodded ruefully. "Pretty much. I soaked what I could with an extinguisher, but it didn't do much good."

After assembling all the facts they'd given him, Bram heaved out a heavy sigh. "Do you still have the key I gave you?" he asked his brother.

Jared took his hands off Kerry long enough to fish the key from his pocket, then hand it to his brother.

"I know this looks bad, Bram, but we just happened to be in the building," Jared told him. "If you ask me, some maniac was trying to kill us. Or at the least, destroy information."

Bram glanced furtively over his shoulder to make sure no one was overhearing their conversation. "We'll have to see what the fire inspector turns up. But I'm inclined to agree with you, Jared. This whole thing is just too coincidental to me."

"So what do you want me and Kerry to do now? She made the 9-1-1 call and the firemen found us in the building trying to save what we could. We're bound to be questioned."

Bram rubbed a thoughtful finger against his jaw. "Just say you two happened to be driving by and you saw the flames through the window. Kerry called 911 and you tried the back door and found it open. Naturally, you two felt it your civic duty to try to put out the flames before the fire department arrived. Got it?"

Jared turned a cheeky grin on Kerry. "My brother, the sheriff. He never breaks a rule."

"Damn it, Jared, I'm not breaking anything!" Bram growled. "Maybe bending. When the fire inspector gets here, I'll give him the full story. I just don't want the general public of Black Arrow knowing my brother was snooping through county courthouse records after working hours!"

Jared affectionately swatted his brother's shoulder. "I was only kidding, Bram. And don't worry. Kerry and I know what to do."

"Good," he countered. "Now you two go ahead and

get out of here. I'll explain to the fire marshal and answer any questions for you.''

''Thanks, brother. If you need us we'll be at my place.''

''Your place?'' Kerry repeated as he shuffled her along to the parking area. ''I have to pick up Peggy.''

''She's with Christa. She's fine. We'll get her later. It's still early and right now we're both wet and filthy. I'm sure you don't want Peggy to see you in this condition.''

Kerry glanced down at her wet, soot-smeared shirt and shorts. He was right. Peggy wouldn't understand seeing her mother looking as though she'd just come out of a war. It might even remind her of the traumatic hours she'd spent trapped in the dirty pipe.

''Okay,'' she agreed. ''I'll follow you in my car.''

Thankfully, the firemen and a few city police who'd gathered at the site had their attention on the burning building and paid no notice to Jared and Kerry leaving the parking lot.

As they headed out of town and into the quiet darkness of the countryside, Kerry began to shake almost uncontrollably and was still shaking when she managed to park in front of Jared's house.

He waited at the car door to help her out and expressed his concern the minute he noticed that she was trembling from head to toe.

''Here, honey, don't try to walk. Let me carry you.''

''Jared, I'm okay. I just got a little chilled,'' she said through chattering teeth.

Ignoring her protest, he bent and swept her up and into his arms, then cradling her tightly against his chest, he maneuvered the both of them through the front gate and on into the house.

In the living room, he placed her on the couch, then switched on a small lamp at one end.

Blinking against the light, she shivered all over again as he sank down close beside her, then carefully cradled her face with both hands.

"You brave little thing. It's no wonder Peggy went into that dark pipe. She's like you—walking into that burning room. I should have taken you out of there right then."

The gentle concern in his voice broke down the last of her defenses. With a needy groan, she flung her arms around his neck and buried her face against his throat. "When I got back from making the call and you were nowhere in sight, I was terrified. I've read about fireballs consuming a room or building in a matter of seconds. You could have been killed!"

The fear in her voice amazed him, humbled him. He'd never had to go looking for women. They'd always come to him. But they'd done so for their own personal pleasure. Not because they cared for him with their heart, the kind of caring that Kerry was showing him now.

"Oh Kerry, were you really that worried about me?"

The warmth of his body was spreading through her, soothing her frazzled nerves and melting away her inhibitions. With her cheek pressed against his neck, she whispered, "I know you think I'm silly, Jared, but the thought of you—I couldn't bear to think I might not ever see you or be with you again."

He'd not expected to hear such an admission from her and his eyes widened with wondrous pleasure as he tilted her face up to his.

"Oh honey, you're not going to have to imagine it. Not now. Not ever," he murmured fervently.

"Jared—"

He didn't allow her to finish. She'd already told him enough. And he'd wanted her for too long to go slowly now.

"Don't talk, sweetheart," he whispered against her lips. "Just let me kiss you. Make love to you. Always...always..."

His words trailed away as the seductive curve of her lips pulled him downward to the velvety warmth of her kiss.

He wrapped his arms around her and lifted her onto his lap. The slightest pressure of his tongue parted her lips and then her teeth. Sweet, mindless pleasure swamped his senses as he invaded the intimate cavern of her mouth.

The thorough search of his lips and tongue was creating havoc inside Kerry. Her heart was slamming against her ribs. Heat was filtering through every limb in her body and collecting like a banked fire at the juncture between her thighs.

When his hands closed over the fabric-covered mounds of her breasts, desire rocketed through her and she arched against him and moaned deep within her throat. To have his fingers touching her skin was what she wanted, needed. Desperately, she caught his hand and directed it under the hem of her wet blouse.

Her invitation sent blood pounding to his head, forcing him to lift his head and drag in several ragged breaths. "Kerry! Kerry! You feel so good in my arms," he groaned with agonizing pleasure. "Let me look at you when I touch you."

Her hands shaking, she helped him deal with the buttons on her blouse. Once it had parted, he pushed it off her shoulders while letting his eyes drink in the way her lacy bra framed her dusky brown breasts like two white hands cupping and fondling their softness.

His mind reeling with anticipation, he unsnapped the front clasp on the delicate garment and slowly pushed the lace aside. Her breasts were small, but pert and perfect, the nipples deep rose brown and turgid with excitement.

Gently, his fingers reached for the beauty before him and stroked the incredibly soft skin. "You're so lovely, Kerry. Too lovely for a man like me."

Her eyes opened to look at him with a mixture of doubt and amusement. "You've had many women, Jared. Don't try to make me believe I'm more special than they were."

But she was special, he thought. If he'd not known it before, he'd learned it tonight when she'd refused to leave his side as the flames roared around them. Her brave and giving heart heightened her physical beauty in a way that, just to look at her, made him ache with pleasure.

With a slight shake of his head, he said, "I've never had a woman like you, Kerry. Not one that looked like you or talked like you. That laughed or smiled or smelled like you. Or—felt like you," he added as his hand moved beneath one breast and cupped its weight like a precious object. "And most of all I've never had a woman with Comanche blood. Like me."

She closed her eyes as her heart hammered inside her chest and hot pleasure dashed along her veins like liquid fire. "You're a smooth-tongued devil, Jared. And I shouldn't be doing this. We shouldn't be doing this. But I—want you," she whispered brokenly, "and I can't seem to stop."

With one hand still on her breast, the other slid up

her throat to cup her chin and tilt her lips toward his. "And I'm not going to let you stop," he said, his voice going rough with passion. "The Great Spirit told Granddad George we're supposed to be together. We can't change our fate."

She tried to turn her head back and forth but his hold on her chin prevented the negative gesture. "You don't believe that," she muttered.

"Let me show you how much I believe it," he said before he closed the last bit of distance between her lips and his.

The hungry kiss left them both gulping for air and Jared aching to connect his body with hers. The unspoken surrender in her heavy-lidded eyes told Jared all he needed to know. She wanted him in the same desperate way and she wasn't going to deny him or herself this chance to quench the desire between them.

Wordlessly, he lifted her in his arms and carried her to the bedroom. There in the small, darkened space, he slowly removed her clothes, then with hurried frustration, he jerked off his boots and tossed his own clothing away.

Although there was no light in the room, the faint rays of moonlight filtering through a pair of windows was enough to illuminate the bed. It was covered with a patchwork quilt and, for a moment, the homey image sent a shaft of panic through Kerry.

Jared would never be her husband. He would never make a family with her, share a house, a home, a future with her. Yet he was the only man she wanted to lie with on a patchwork quilt.

Sensing her hesitation, he paused, his hands lingering on the tiny circle of her bare waist. "Kerry honey, is this okay with you? Do you want us to stop right here and now?''

Lifting her face to his, she searched his solemn gaze and as she did, something in his eyes, some long, lonely need spoke to her and settled the last vestige of her doubts.

''No,'' she whispered fervently. ''I don't want us to stop. I want to be your woman, Jared.'' Now and for always, she silently added.

With a grunt of satisfaction, he tossed her and himself backwards and onto the wide bed. The mattress bounced beneath their weight and he chuckled wickedly as the front of her collided softly with him.

''I know we don't have much time,'' he said as his hand slid possessively over the curve of her hip. ''But don't ask me to hurry, Kerry. I've wanted you for too long to rush this.''

Her hands came up to cradle his face. ''How long?'' she wanted to know.

His hands were slipping around to her back, drawing her tight against his hot naked skin. The contact sent shivers of pleasure pulsing through every inch of her body.

''I think I wanted you from the first time I saw you with a coffeepot in your hand, weaving your way through the tables at Woody's Café.''

''You're such a liar,'' she said, but there was a smile on her face that brightened his heart.

Pressing his forehead against hers, he murmured, ''I would never lie to you, Kerry. Believe that and remember it. Okay?''

At this moment she was drunk on desire for this man, she realized. She would believe anything he said. Except I love you. She wasn't that far gone—yet.

"Yes," she whispered. "I'll remember."

Her answer appeared to give him a great sense of relief. With a sudden chuckle, he rolled the both of them so that she was resting on top of him and his laughing eyes were looking into hers.

"Now I have you where I want you," he said thickly.

Feeling wanton and oh so wanted, she brushed her breasts against his chest. "You might not be thinking that—in a few minutes."

Sliding his hand into her hair, he cupped the back of her head and tugged her face down to his. "You talk way too much, my woman."

He closed the last gap between their lips and in a matter of seconds the desire between them flared as he tasted her mouth, her throat and the budded nipples of her breasts. At the same time her small hands explored the corded muscles of his arms, chest and washboard belly.

Jared had told her he didn't want to hurry this time between them and he'd meant it. But her soft lips and searching hands were quickly changing his plans, building a fire in his loins that threatened to consume him.

He'd never wanted a woman like this. So much, so swiftly that his mind was emptied of everything but her taste, her smell and the feel of her warm, pliant body draped over his.

"Kerry...I can't wait," he spoke through gritted teeth. "I've got to have you. Now!"

He started to roll her beneath him, but she pressed his shoulders back against the patchwork quilt. "Let me love you like this, Jared," she whispered hoarsely.

Jared wasn't sure if it was at this moment that he

lost his heart or later, as the silky heat of her body slipped over his manhood. Either way, by the time her cries of release were joined by his own guttural groans of pleasure, he knew he had to have this woman until the very end of his days.

Chapter Ten

"Kerry, if last night didn't convince you about Jared Colton, I don't know what will."

Enola's remark had Kerry looking up from the squash vine she was searching to the opposite end of the garden where her mother was picking green beans.

Could her mother tell she'd spent part of the night making passionate love to Black Arrow's newest hero? Kerry wondered. Maybe the pleasure he'd given her was still on her face. It wouldn't surprise her, she'd felt as if she'd been glowing all day.

"What is that supposed to mean?" she asked, trying to sound totally at ease instead of dreading another one of her mother's lectures.

Enola raised up from her bent position and jammed both fists against her back. "I shouldn't have to explain, Kerry. The courthouse is on fire and he drags you inside to help him try to put it out. If the man cared one whit for you, he wouldn't have allowed you to be anywhere near that burning building.''

Even though Kerry desperately wanted to jump to Jared's defense, there wasn't much she could say. She couldn't explain what had really taken place last night. Not when Bram had asked them to keep the real story under wraps. And even if she could tell her mother, she wouldn't. It would worry Enola sick to think someone had intentionally meant to harm her and Jared.

''Jared would never put my life in danger,'' she said. ''Have you forgotten that he risked his own life to save your granddaughter's?''

Enola glanced over her shoulder to a spot in the lawn where Peggy was pushing Claws and a bewildered Fred in a doll buggy. In spite of the playful scene, the woman's lips were set in a grim line. ''I haven't forgotten. But he's used your daughter to get to you. Don't try to deny it.''

Kerry reached for the yellow squash hidden beneath a wide spiky leaf resting on the ground. ''I'm not going to deny anything, Mom. How Jared and I got together isn't important. I'm only going to tell you that you might as well get used to him being in mine and Peggy's life.''

Enola stared at her as though she'd just uttered a filthy word. Forgetting the bucket of beans at her feet, the woman marched toward Kerry. ''Have you lost your mind, daughter? Have you forgotten what Damon did to you?''

How could I, you've been reminding me of it every day for the past four years. Out loud, she answered, ''I'm trying to, Mom. I want to have a normal life again. Not waste it with bitterness and mistrust.''

Enola's head swung back and forth in disbelief.

"Don't tell me you trust Jared Colton? I know you have more sense than that."

I would never lie to you, Kerry.

Jared's whispered words filtered through her mind and she realized she did trust him. She had to. Because she'd fallen in love with him.

That conclusion hadn't come to her suddenly last night, but rather in gradual stages today as she'd worked at her desk. Slowly she'd come to realize that for the past four years she'd been going around with her heart and mind closed to any sort of love and happiness. Maybe she'd convinced herself that she didn't deserve another chance after the horrible mistake she'd made with Damon. Or maybe she'd simply been too downright scared to even think about trying again. Either way, each minute, each hour she'd spent with Jared since Peggy's mishap had changed her.

Now, just to think about the future without Jared in it, was like imagining a life without sunshine.

"So far Jared hasn't given me any reason not to trust him, Mom."

Enola snorted. "No. He's too smart for that. He'll dangle you along until it's time for him to go. Then you'll be left behind. Just like all the other women he's had." The shake of her head made the turquoise thunderbird earrings dangling from her ears appear to take off in flight. "What has he promised you?"

Her face devoid of emotion, Kerry turned away from her mother and gathered up what squash she'd picked so far. "That's between Jared and I."

"In other words, he hasn't promised you anything," she said dryly. "Well, at least he's being honest up to a point."

No, Kerry thought. After the two of them had made

love last night, he'd not promised her undying devotion or a beautiful home with a picket fence. She'd not expected him to. For him, their relationship was only beginning. And even though she already loved him, she would have to be patient, to wait and see if he wanted a future with her.

Dumping the squash into a five-gallon bucket, Kerry turned toward the house. "You must have a very low opinion of me."

The pained look on Enola's face said Kerry might as well have stabbed her. "Kerry," she said, her tone suddenly placating, "I only want you to be happy."

"Like you've been all these years, Mom?"

Enola's mouth fell open and she stared at her for long moments, then wordlessly she walked back over to the row of beans and resumed her picking as though she'd never heard the question.

Her heart heavy, Kerry called to her daughter and headed into the house.

Dusk was falling when Jared parked behind the Arrow Feed and Grain store. Since it was past closing time, he expected to find his sister Willow inside tallying up the cash register, but instead he spotted her tall, strong figure rolling a spool of goucho wire through the double doors of a storage shed, which was built onto the side of the main building.

Hurrying over to help her, he took her by the shoulders and set her to one side out of the way. "Let a man do this, little sis."

Willow wiped at the messy strands of hair that had escaped from her long black braid. "Where were you hours ago, when I had to load two hundred cedar fence posts for one of my customers?"

He gave the spool one last kick with his boot to shove it in a space next to a stack of metal fence posts. "Working, honey. I'm like you, I have to make a living."

She chuckled as she tugged a pair of leather gloves from her hands. "I know how you work. You stand around and point while your crew does all the sweating. Then you get paid the big bucks."

Jared slung his arm around his sister's shoulder and squeezed. "That's why I went to college. You know, it's still not too late for you."

Willow shook her head. "That's just not me. The Arrow Feed and Grain has always been in the Colton family and I'm going to see that it stays that way. Besides, Gran needs me."

Jared released his hold on her and Willow closed the double doors and locked them. As the two of them headed through a back entrance of the feed store, Jared asked, "Speaking of our grandmother, where is Gran?"

"I sent her upstairs about an hour ago to lie down, why?"

"I thought I might talk to her, but if she's not feeling well I guess it'll have to wait," Jared told her.

Willow glanced at him as they continued to walk to the front of the store where the cash register was located. "I think her blood pressure is up. Her face was red and she hardly had the energy to walk across the floor. But she refuses to go to the doctor."

"Does she still insist on helping you here in the store every day?"

Willow grimaced. "She wouldn't have it any other way. And you know how stubborn she can be. What did you want to talk to her about?"

Jared watched his sister open the cash register and carefully pull out the take for the day. The stacks of bills were thick and he knew the store's success was due to the long hard hours she put in to make sure her customers' needs were met.

He leaned his hip against the counter while she began to count. "I guess you heard about the fire last night."

Willow let out a short laugh. "I doubt there's a person in Black Arrow who didn't hear all those fire trucks last night. I thought the whole town must have been on fire. Bram called and told me a little about it."

"Uh—did he happen to tell you about me and Kerry?"

"Very little. Only that you two saw it and tried to put it out before the fire crew got there. What's that got to do with Gran?"

"Probably nothing. Except that a stranger was seen at the courthouse earlier this week asking to go through records pertaining to our family."

"A crazy coyote is stalking our family. All of us must watch out for his tracks."

The sound of his great-grandfather's voice caused Jared to whirl around. "Hellfire, George! What are you doing sneaking up on us like that?"

The old man lifted his bony hands in a gesture that was both innocent and amusing. "What do you expect an Indian to do, make a lot of damn noise?"

Jared heaved out a breath and arched an accusing eye at his sister. "Why didn't you warn me he was around?"

"He hitched a ride into town with his neighbor, Annie McCrary, because he had a feeling Gloria wasn't feeling up to snuff. He's supposed to be upstairs watching out for his daughter,'' Willow said as she concentrated on her money count.

"She's asleep," George said. "And I want to know what we're gonna have for supper."

"Pizza. There's two in the freezer. All you have to do is put them in the oven," Willow told him.

"I know how to cook, missy," George retorted.

Taking pity on his sister, Jared took his great-grandfather by the shoulder and headed him toward a back staircase that led up to Willow's apartment. "Come on, Granddad, I'll help you. And maybe while the pizza's baking you can give me some answers."

Upstairs in the compact kitchen, Jared found the frozen disks of pizza, ignored the part about preheating the oven, and tossed them straight on the rack. After that, he set George at the table with a long-necked beer.

Willow would frown on him for giving the old man the bit of alcohol, but Jared understood that his great-grandfather wanted to be treated like a man, not a child.

"You were at the courthouse last night with your woman," George said as though he'd known even before anyone had told him. "And someone tried to burn the place down with you in it."

That pretty much summed it up, Jared thought, as he twisted off the cap on his own beer. Aloud, he said, "We don't know that for sure, Granddad."

"Maybe you and Bram don't. But I do."

The beer in Jared's hand paused halfway to his mouth as he cautiously eyed his great-grandfather. "If you know that much, then you must know what this person wants."

George closed his eyes and scratched the top of his head. "No. Except that he means to hurt us in some way."

"Us" meaning the Coltons, Jared silently translated his great-grandfather's words. "Do you think Gran would know what any of this might be about?"

The old man narrowed his eyes shrewdly at Jared. "I wouldn't ask her."

Grimacing with frustration, Jared asked, "Why? If she can help solve this thing."

"It would only worry her. To make her remember the past only hurts her. And she's too fragile now."

Old George was probably right, Jared thought. Unlike most people who'd reached their eighties, Gloria refused to talk about the bygone days. Especially the time she'd spent in Nevada. Even if she'd been up and about this evening she probably wouldn't have told Jared anything.

"You make it sound like Gran has something to hide," Jared said thoughtfully.

George's wrinkled face creased into a cagey grin. "Everyone has something to hide. Even you, my son."

Jared let out a good-natured chuckle. "I've never tried to hide the kind of man I am."

The old Comanche didn't reply. Instead he took a long drink of beer and stared across the room as though he were looking at the vast Oklahoma plains, back in a time when his ancestors drove mighty herds of horses over great grasslands and took their raids as far south as the Texas coast.

After a minute or two had passed Jared decided his great-grandfather's mind had wandered completely off their conversation so he rose to his feet to check on the pizza.

"You are trying to hide what's in here."

George's unexpected words had Jared turning away

from the oven to see his great-grandfather thumping a fist against his chest.

Knowing he'd probably pay dearly for this, Jared asked it anyway. "What's that supposed to mean?"

"You love the woman and her little dove, but you want to hide it away and keep it to yourself."

For a moment Jared felt as though he'd had the wind knocked out of him. Sure, George had prophesied that the Great Spirit had meant for Jared and Kerry to be together and the foretelling remark had come true in a sense last night. But Jared had not expected George to be so perceptive about what was going on in his heart.

"And how do you know that I love Kerry?"

George grunted with amusement. "Because I can see that you've changed."

Jared rolled his eyes. "You haven't even seen me in several days. You don't know what I've been doing."

Another grunt sounded from the old man. "I don't have to see you to know what's been happening to you."

Apparently not, Jared thought. Then wondered a bit sheepishly if his great-grandfather had somehow envisioned the passionate love he and Kerry had made last night. Just the thought of the totally selfless pleasure she'd given him still had the power to curl his toes.

Walking back over to the table, Jared sank down in the chair across from George. "Okay, Granddad. You're right. I do love Kerry. I never thought I'd say that about any woman, but I'm saying it now."

The old man's wrinkled face took on a pleased look. "So why are you scared?"

Jared wasn't going to bother asking him how he'd recognized his grandson's fear. That part of it didn't matter anymore. And for some reason it was reassuring to know that George understood him. Maybe even more than he understood himself.

Sighing, Jared ran a hand through his thick black hair. He hadn't come to Willow's this evening to get a lecture on women from his great-grandfather. In fact, he was still mostly in shock over his newfound love for Kerry. All day he'd been thinking, wondering how he was going to fit Kerry and Peggy into his life. He'd never planned to be a husband or a father. He'd never expected to want to be those things. But now he was suddenly seeing the world through different eyes.

"I've never had anyone of my own, Granddad. Not for keeps."

"You haven't wanted anybody for keeps," George wisely pointed out.

Jared shrugged with resignation. "The minute a man gets hooked up with a woman, he has to start worrying about losing her."

Clearly disappointed, George shook his head. "Losing a woman isn't the worst thing that could ever happen to a man."

Jared arched a brow at him. "I suppose now you're going to tell me what the worst thing is," he said wearily.

George directed his foretelling gaze straight at his grandson. "The worst thing for a man is not ever having a woman."

The old man's simple statement was so far from what Jared expected, he could only stare at him. Then slowly as the words settled deep inside him, it was as though George had suddenly pulled back a curtain and he could see how his life had been up until now and how it could be, had to be with Kerry.

"What's going on? Are you two guys letting the pizza burn?"

Willow's question snapped Jared out of his trance. "No, sis. But now that you're here to take over I have to be going."

His sister was clearly disappointed. "Oh, but aren't you going to stay long enough to eat?"

Rising to his feet, Jared patted his great-grandfather on the shoulder. "Thanks sis, but I gotta run. Tell Gran I said hello."

Outside, he climbed into his truck and pulled onto the street with intentions of heading straight to the WindWalker place. He had to talk to Kerry. Really talk to her. But he desperately needed a shower first. He didn't want to give Enola one more excuse to dislike him.

Less than an hour later, he was shaved, showered and dressed in clean Levi's and a blue cotton shirt. When he pulled to a stop in front of the WindWalker house, he noticed it was nearly nine-thirty. It was rather late to be calling, but lights filtering from the living room assured him the women were still up and about.

A few short moments after he knocked Kerry came to the door. When she saw that it was him, a look of surprise and joy crossed her face. "Jared! I didn't expect to see you this evening."

The sight of her sweet face and gentle smile filled him with a pleasure that was all new to Jared. She wasn't just a beautiful woman he found attractive, she was the women he loved and that made everything different.

"You didn't really expect me to stay away, did you?"

Kerry glanced back over her shoulder, then quietly

stepped out to join him. The second she was standing beside him on the dark porch, Jared yanked her into his arms and covered her lips in a totally consuming kiss.

The connection was brief, but hot enough to leave them both dazed and gasping for breath. Kerry clung to the front of his shirt while his hands roamed her back and took pleasure in the soft, rounded curves of her body.

"Oh honey, I've missed you," he said. "I had to see you tonight. I couldn't wait."

"Jared," she said on a rush of breath. "We need—"

"To talk," he explained. "Though God knows how I wish we could be together. Like we were last night."

Heat suffused her cheeks as her eyes clung to his face. "I've been thinking constantly about that. About you and me—"

"You don't regret it, do you?" he anxiously interrupted.

"No."

He released a huge breath. "Thank God. Last night, after you went home, I was afraid you'd start having second thoughts."

"No," she repeated.

His hands gently framed her face. "We didn't get to talk much last night before you left my house. That's why I couldn't let another day go past without seeing you." He peered over her shoulder toward the door leading into the house. "What about now? Do you need to tend to Peggy?"

"She's already in bed asleep. And my mother is lying down reading. Do you want to go into the house?"

He shook his head. "What I want to say to you—I want us to be entirely alone, okay?"

The urgency in his voice put her heartbeat in rapid motion. "Jared, is something wrong?"

He reached for her hand. "Let's go sit in my truck," he said.

Kerry allowed him to lead her out to his company vehicle, then help her climb into the cab. Once he was inside with her, he immediately pulled her into his arms and kissed her for long, dizzying moments.

When he finally broke the contact, Kerry drew in a ragged breath and rested her cheek against his shoulder. "I thought you said you wanted to talk."

"I want to do everything with you, Kerry," he murmured. "Funny how much I know that now."

The weight of his hands, the scent of his skin and the hard warmth of his body soothed her, filled her with a quiet pleasure that worked itself all the way to her heart.

"I don't understand, Jared."

His husky chuckle slithered across her cheek. "I'm sure you don't. I didn't understand it myself until…we made love last night. And even then I didn't quite want to admit it to myself."

She waited for him to go on and when he didn't, she tilted her head back far enough to see his face. "Admit what?"

A smile settled over his features. "That I love you."

She stared at him in stunned fascination. He'd said the words so easily and with such confidence that it was difficult not to believe him. Yet it couldn't be true, she thought. Jared Colton couldn't love her.

A long, pent-up breath rushed past her lips. "Jared— last night—if you're saying this just because—"

Her words halted as he gently grasped her face between his hands. "Last night was—I've never shared anything so special with anyone, Kerry. But that's not why I told you that I love you. I told you because I mean it. Because I want you to know how I feel about you."

Her ears had to believe what she was hearing, yet her heart wasn't so easily convinced. It was still cowering behind its scarred past.

"I'm—I don't know what to think," she told him. "I'm not even sure I believe you."

He groaned. "Kerry, remember when I told you I would never lie to you?"

She nodded, which immediately brought a smile to his face.

"Then believe me now."

"A few moments ago you said you didn't want to admit something to yourself. Were you talking about—loving me?"

He moved his hands to her shoulders. "Like I said before, Kerry, I'm not going to lie to you. So yeah, it was tough for me to admit to myself that I'd finally run into a woman I couldn't take lightly."

She was suddenly overwhelmed with the idea that maybe what he was saying was true. He really did love her. "Oh Jared. You could have anyone you wanted. Why me?"

With a hand at the back of her head, he pressed his cheek against hers. "My little sweetheart. I don't want just anybody. You've ruined me. Now the only woman I'll ever want is you."

Tears suddenly clogged her throat, making it impossible to speak. With a tiny sob, she flung her arms around his neck and buried her face against his chest.

"Kerry? Are you crying?" he asked in disbelief.

When she didn't answer, he tipped up her chin, then groaned as he spotted the tears on her face.

Using his forefinger, he gently wiped at the salty tracks on her cheeks. "Tell me, sweetheart. What's wrong? Are you trying to let me down easy?"

That caught her attention and she stared at him in confusion. "What do you mean?"

"Are you trying to tell me that you don't love me back? That I'm wasting my time here?"

Her gaze dropped to where his shirt veed against his throat. "We haven't known each other very long," she murmured.

"We've known each other for years," he argued.

"Only from a distance."

His hand stroked her hair. "And that was enough for me."

The simple statement went straight to her heart. "Oh Jared, this is all wrong. I wasn't supposed to fall in love with a man like you."

His hands were suddenly gripping her shoulder. "Say that again."

Kerry dared to lift her eyes to his. "I wasn't supposed to fall in love with a man like you."

A slow, euphoric smile spread across his face. "Then you do love me."

"I'm afraid I do."

He appeared to miss the misery in her voice. Instead he showered kisses over her cheeks, down her neck, then back up to her lips, where he whispered, "Kerry, Kerry. Why would you be afraid?"

Sighing, she turned away from the temptation of his lips. "Jared, don't you understand? I've spent the past four years trying to put my life back together. I didn't think I'd ever want to be near another man. Now you've come along—''

With a hand at the side of her face, he urged her to look at him. "You're going to be next to me for the rest of your life, Kerry. You might as well get ready for that."

Torment filled her eyes. "Maybe you think that way right now—at this moment. But you're a wanderer, Jared. You've already said you'll be leaving Black Arrow once your job is finished. You haven't changed your mind about that, have you?"

He eased her back so that he could look her fully in the face. "No," he said after a moment. "But what does that have to do with you loving me and me loving you?"

Closing her eyes, she stifled down another groan of torment. "My home is here, Jared. Or were you just planning on us having a long-distance relationship?"

"Like hell," he cursed. "Wherever I go, you go. You and Peggy."

Her heart sank like a dead weight. "No, Jared. That's not the kind of life I want or need. It's not the kind of life I want for my daughter. I want us to have a real home, a rooted home."

Jared released a heavy sigh, then slowly eased back in the seat. "What do you expect from me, Kerry? To give up my job? I worked like hell to get my engineering degree. It's not something I want to just toss away. And let's face it, we can't live on love alone. I want to be able to give you financial security."

Kerry didn't know it was possible to feel so deliriously happy one minute and deflated the next. Jared loved her! Just knowing that thrilled her, filled her heart with wondrous joy. Yet her eyes were open enough to see that he had no intentions of giving her the kind of home she needed for herself and for Peggy. Why hadn't she reminded herself of that fact last night before she'd made love with him, she asked herself bitterly.

Because once he'd touched you, that was it. You were like a little lamb lost and fool enough to think you'd find a home in the arms of the big bad wolf.

She sighed. "Surely you don't think I'd be selfish enough to want you to give up your job?"

"Then what do you want me to do?"

Regret plunged deep inside her as she realized there was nothing he could do or say to break down the wall of differences between them. "Forget about me. About us and last night."

He didn't say anything and after a while, when the silence became too much for her to bear, she forced herself to look at him.

"I can't. I won't," he said with grim resolution. "I don't know about you, Kerry, but I've never felt like this about anyone before. You can't ask me to give you up."

She covered her face with both hands. "Oh Jared, this just isn't going to work," she mumbled. "We'll only make each other miserable if we try."

His brows inched upward as though he couldn't believe what she was telling him. "If that's the way you feel, then why did you sleep with me last night?" he asked angrily. "Why didn't you make it clear you just wanted a one-night stand?"

Dropping her hands, she stared at him in stunned disbelief. "Is that what you think about me? Is that the sort of woman you think I am? I just told you that I loved you!"

His lips twisted. "Sure," he said cynically. "You love me so much you'll follow me to the ends of the earth."

"And you love me so much you'll forget about traveling the globe to work for some rich gas or oil company," she shot back at him. As soon as the last word died on her lips, she regretted losing her temper. She didn't want to hurt Jared. She loved him. But she couldn't see what good that was going to do either of them now.

She reached for his hand and felt a sense of relief when his fingers clasped tightly around hers. "Oh Jared," she pleaded, "I don't want us to be angry at each other. We've just now found each other."

He couldn't stay angry with her, Jared realized. Not with her hand clinging to his and her eyes begging for him to understand.

He stroked a hand through her silky hair. "Then don't ask me to forget you, Kerry. We'll work this out somehow. Trust me."

"I—told my mother this evening that she had to get used to you being in my life now."

Surprised by her admission, he asked, "What did she think about that? Not much I'm sure."

"She thinks I'm crazy to trust you. Am I?"

Jared drew her back into the circle of his arms. "I'm the one who's crazy. I'd marry you tomorrow if you'd say the word."

Instead of being thrilled at his mention of marriage, she was terrified to think of herself as Mrs. Jared Colton. She'd trustingly handed her heart to a man before and he'd eventually stomped it. A marriage license was no guarantee that Jared would be any different.

"Jared, this is too soon. I have Peggy to think about—"

"I adore Peggy. I want to be her father. I want to be your husband. What more do I need to say?"

At this moment Kerry wasn't sure what she needed from him. Even if he said he'd forget his job and stay right here in Black Arrow, she wouldn't be convinced they could make it as a family.

"There's nothing you can say, Jared," she said in a raw, husky voice. "It's not your fault. It's mine. I'm just not ready to jump in with both feet."

"Then I'll have to do everything I can to make you ready," he said gently.

She pressed a kiss on his cheek, then pushed herself away from him. "It's getting late. I've got to go in."

"All right," he reluctantly agreed, "but we'll take this up tomorrow night at my house. I'll cook supper for you and Peggy."

"You're not playing fair, Jared."

Grinning sexily, he leaned forward and planted a soft kiss on her lips. "I have no intention of playing fair, Kerry. So get ready."

"Jared—"

The rest of her protest was cut off by a hungry kiss that left Kerry's senses reeling, crumbling beneath a hot weight of desire.

"All right, I'll see you tomorrow night," she promised once he lifted his head. But as she quickly climbed out of the truck and headed into the house, she wondered if she'd lost her mind, along with her heart.

Chapter Eleven

The next evening Jared was frying T-bone steaks when Bram entered the kitchen by way of the back door. One glance at his tired face told Jared something other than a brotherly chat was on his mind.

"Hey, an unexpected visit from my brother," Jared greeted him. "What's up?"

Bram pulled out a chair from the kitchen table and straddled it. "I'm on my way home to the ranch. I thought I'd stop by and clue you in on the fire."

Jared turned away from the sizzling skillet to face his brother. "Has the fire inspector come to any conclusions?"

"He wound up the investigation this afternoon and although it will be a while before he makes any public statement, he's told me it was a clear case of arson. In fact, he said there wasn't even an attempt to hide the origin of the fire. Someone splashed gasoline everywhere then tossed on a few burning candles.''

Even though Jared had pretty much suspected the fire had been set, hearing the facts from Bram sent a cold chill to the pit of his stomach.

"Hell, Bram, what's going on here? Who would want to hurt me and Kerry?''

"We don't know if the arson was meant to harm you two. The perpetrator might not have been aware that you two were in the courthouse.''

Jared cursed. ''You don't believe that any more than I do. The bastard knew we were there. He couldn't have missed the light or our voices. He was only a room away from us!''

Bram swiped a hand across his face. ''Yeah. You're right. I think there was real criminal intent here,'' he admitted in a weary tone. ''I'm just not sure if the fire was directed toward you and Kerry or if it was only set to destroy county records. Or both.''

Suddenly remembering the steaks, Jared turned back to the cookstove and flipped the contents of the skillet.

"I don't get it, Bram. Kerry and I went through most of the birth and marriage certificates in the Colton family and we didn't see anything out of the ordinary. Why would anyone want to destroy our family records?''

"Why does anyone want to destroy information,'' he said grimly. ''To cover up something.''

"Yeah. But what?'' Jared countered. ''I went by the feed store last night to talk to Gran about it. I was hoping she could shed some light on this whole thing. But she wasn't feeling well and had gone to bed.''

"I doubt she would have told you anything.'' Bram

replied. "She's always been tight-lipped. Especially about her younger years."

"I can't understand why," Jared said as he forked one of the seared T-bones onto a warmed platter. "She's been a widow for what, sixty years or more now? You'd think she could talk about the man without breaking apart."

Bram rose from the chair to join Jared at the stove. "You think this has something to do with our grandfather?"

Jared shrugged. "Hell Bram, I'm just guessing. I really can't see how it could be connected to him. Gran is eighty years old and as far as we know she's never heard anything from his family. We don't even know if he had any family."

Bram took a few moments to mull over Jared's suggestion before he spoke. "That's true enough. And I'm not so sure I want to be the one to question Gran about this," he admitted. "Are you going to try again?"

Jared reached up to a cabinet to his left and pulled down three plates. "George says I shouldn't. He says it won't gain anything and will only upset her."

Bram cast a curious look at his younger brother. "George? What does Granddad know about any of this?"

Jared snorted. "Are you kidding? That old man knows everything." He glanced at Bram. "Did you tell him about the fire—that someone tried to fry me and Kerry?"

"Lord, no! I haven't even spoken to him in several days. When did you?"

Jared pulled out a drawer of silverware and picked out three of everything. "Last night at the feed store.

He says a crazy coyote is stalking the Colton family. And that we all need to watch out for his tracks.''

Bram chuckled. ''Jared, the man is ninety-seven years old. He believes he's some damn Comanche medicine man or prophet, or something.''

''Try chief,'' Jared said dryly.

''Well, whatever, he couldn't have known about you and Kerry. The only people who know you were in the building are the firefighters and the fire inspector.''

Maybe Bram didn't believe in George's spouts of wisdom, but Jared wasn't about to dismiss their great-grandfather's words. Especially after George's uncanny perception about him and Kerry.

Carrying the plates and silverware to the table, he began to place the settings on three placemats. ''Did you have any trouble convincing the fire inspector that Kerry and I were innocent victims?''

''No. You were there legally. You had my permission. It would have been idiotic for you two to set a fire, then call the fire department and remain there to try to put it out. Besides, the inspector knows I'd tell him the truth. Even if it meant incriminating my own brother.''

''Thanks,'' Jared said with a wry chuckle as he headed back to the cookstove and the sizzling skillet of steak. ''I always knew if I got in a pinch you'd step up to bat for me.''

''You're not in a pinch, so you'd better thank God, and me, for that,'' he told him, then glanced pointedly at the table set for three. ''Are you having guests for supper, or did you put out two extra plates for me?'' Bram asked.

Jared chuckled again. ''Not hardly. Kerry and her daughter are coming out tonight.'' With a broad grin, he glanced at his wristwatch. "In fact, they'll be here in just a few minutes."

Folding his arms across his chest, Bram leaned against the cabinet counter as he studied his brother. "Hmm. Cooking supper for a woman. And her child. This is a new one for you."

"Get used to it, Bram. I'm going to make Kerry my wife."

Totally stunned, Bram stared at him. "I knew you were attracted to the woman, but marriage—hell, I never thought I'd see this day. You a husband!"

Jared grimaced. "What do you mean by that? You're older than me and you still haven't hitched yourself up with a woman."

Ignoring the personal jab, Bram said, "If you ask me, this is all rather sudden. What does Kerry think about this? Has she agreed to marry you?"

Jared opened the oven door and tested the baking potatoes for doneness. "No. But she will."

"What's the matter?" Bram asked wryly. "Losing your touch?"

Jared shut the oven door, then raised up to glare at his brother. "The woman has been hurt. She's a little leery."

"Of you? Or marriage in general?"

Jared sighed. "Both, I expect. She thinks I'll drag her and Peggy from state to state and she doesn't want that. She wants a permanent home."

"Most women want to stay put, Jared. Surely you can understand that."

Jared nodded glumly. "Yeah, I can understand it. But what am I supposed to do? I can't just toss my job away and settle for a menial job that would do well to cover the monthly cost of living, much less savings or luxuries. I don't want that kind of life for Kerry and Peggy. I want to be able to give them everything they want and deserve.''

Bram studied him for long moments. ''I may be crazy, but I actually believe you're in love.''

A wide, charmed smile spread over Jared's face. ''Bram, I never thought I'd ever meet a woman like Kerry. I wasn't even hunting one like her, because I didn't think they existed. But everything about her is wonderful. Her smile, her walk and talk and the way her little hand hangs on to mine like I'm some brave Comanche warrior that will always keep her safe.'' He stopped and shook his head in amazement. ''Do you know she wouldn't leave me alone that night in the burning room? The ceiling could have fallen at any moment, but she was more concerned about my safety. And I don't have to tell you what a dedicated mother she is to Peggy.''

Bram grinned. ''Yeah. And I can also see that you're pretty hooked on the woman.'' His expression sobered. ''So you need to make this work, Jared. No matter what you have to do.''

Jared closed his eyes and pinched the bridge of his nose. ''That's what worries me, Bram. I don't know what to do. And it scares me to death to think I might lose Kerry.''

Bram patted his brother's shoulder. ''You'll know the right thing to do when the time comes. And who knows,'' he added with a teasing grin, ''maybe Grand-dad can give you some of his sage wisdom.''

Jared dropped his hand and shot him an annoyed look. ''Don't make fun of George. I'm telling you, Bram, he knows things. He may sound kooky at times, but he sees this stuff before it happens. It wouldn't hurt any of us to listen more closely to what he has to say."

Bram started to laugh, but the serious look on Jared's face stopped him. "Jared, what's happened to you? You were always the first one to poke fun at Granddad's visions and predictions."

Jared let out a long breath. "I don't know, Bram. I guess love changes a man. It opens his eyes. Or at least, it has mine. Everything seems different to me now. I never knew the sky was so blue or the grass so green. Maybe you ought to try it."

The suggestion was enough to get Bram headed toward the door. "I'm a happy man just like I am. So I'm gonna get out of here before your little honey arrives."

"Hey Bram," Jared called to him as he stepped out the door. "Let me know if you get any leads on the arsonist. I'd like to see him behind bars."

"You and me both, brother." He lifted his hand in farewell and shut the door behind him.

Jared turned back to finishing the last of the meal and while he worked, his mind kept turning over the news Bram had given him. Someone had blatantly set fire to the courthouse. Not only that, he'd set it in the very room next to where he and Kerry had been working. Why hadn't they heard him moving about? he wondered. And how had the person gotten in without being noticed? He hoped to heck Bram could figure it out. The idea that someone was out for him or anyone that he loved chilled him.

Ten minutes later, he was taking a loaf of buttered Italian bread out of the oven, when he heard Kerry's knock on the front door.

He hurried out to greet her and was totally bowled

over the moment he opened the door and spotted her on the threshold. She was wearing a filmy dress printed in small pink and burgundy flowers. The neck was scooped low and the bodice clung to her body, outlining the pert curves of her breasts. Her hair was pulled back on the sides and fastened with silver barrettes. The extra touch of makeup on her eyes and lips gave her an exotic, tempting look and the urge to pull her into his arms and kiss the cherry color from her mouth hit him like a hammer. But with little Peggy standing at her side, he had to control himself.

"Hello," he greeted her, while pushing open the door to allow them entry. "You're right on time. I just took the bread out of the oven."

As they stepped past him, he leaned forward and planted a swift kiss on Kerry's cheek. Color immediately bloomed in her face and she cast him a shy smile.

"I'm glad we haven't kept you waiting," she murmured.

"It was worth it," he said softly as his eyes devoured the sight of her. "You look gorgeous tonight."

"Thank you."

His gaze lingered on her lips for one last moment, then he turned his attention to Peggy. The little girl was dressed in a blue short set and her wavy black hair was pulled into a bouncy ponytail atop her head.

As Jared squatted on his heels, and drew the child into the circle of his arm, emotions swelled in his chest. He'd never thought much about being a father or how it might feel to have a child of his own, but Peggy had changed all that.

"How's my best girl? Have you missed me?" he asked.

She nodded fiercely. "I've been telling Mama to call

you, 'cause I wanted to see you. But she says you have lots of things to do and that we can't be bothering you.''

He shot a frown up at Kerry, then turned an apologetic smile on Peggy. "I'm sorry I haven't had a chance to see you in a few days, Chenoa. But I haven't forgotten you. Next to your mother, you're my very best girl."

A wide grin spread across her pretty little face and she curled her arms around his neck and kissed his cheek.

Above her head, Jared glanced at Kerry, who was smiling indulgently at the two of them. "Think I'm forgiven?" he asked Kerry.

She laughed softly. "I think she'd forgive you anything."

Chuckling, Jared rose to his feet with Peggy perched carefully on his arm. "Come on, little dove," he said, "let's eat and then we'll go outside and I'll push you in the swing."

In the kitchen, the table was already laid out with tossed salad, baked potatoes, steak and hot bread. Jared found a big cooking pot and turned it upside down in a chair for Peggy to use as a booster seat. After he carefully seated her and then Kerry, he went to the cabinet and poured iced tea for the adults and a glass of milk for Peggy.

"If you cooked this yourself, I'm very impressed," Kerry told him when he'd taken his own seat at the end of the table. "Are you sure Willow didn't do this?"

He laughed at her suggestion. "Willow's a tomboy, always has been. I can cook anything she can. Besides, there's nothing to it. Anybody can throw a piece of meat in a skillet.''

''It takes a little more work than that to make all this,'' she said gesturing toward the food on the table.

''Mama makes spaghetti,'' Peggy spoke up, ''and it's good. She knows how to cook everything.''

Jared's brows lifted suggestively as he looked at Kerry. ''Sounds like I'm in for all kinds of treats.''

His double-edged remark had her clearing her throat. ''I'm not so sure about that,'' she murmured, amazed at how easily he could turn her cheeks beet red.

''Well,'' he said to Peggy, ''I doubt this food is as good as your mama's, but maybe you'll like it.''

He passed a bowl to Kerry who immediately began to fill Peggy's plate.

''Fred likes spaghetti, but Claws don't like it too much,'' Peggy continued. ''He likes tuna.''

''I'll bet he likes tuna,'' Jared said with a chuckle, then asked the child, ''You haven't been following Fred out of the yard anymore have you?''

Peggy shook her head back and forth. ''Uh-uh. I don't want to get lost again. And Claws is too little to go out of the yard. He might get hurt. So I stay there with him.''

Jared reached over and patted her cheek. ''That's my good girl.''

For the next half hour the three of them enjoyed the meal while Peggy took charge of the conversation. Jared had to admit he was entranced with the child. He'd not known someone so young could be so bright and talkative. And as he watched her animated expressions it was so easy to imagine her growing into a beautiful young woman. His daughter. He wanted to give her the best of everything. He wanted her to have every chance to follow her dreams, to become a doctor, lawyer, or whatever her heart desired. And most of all he wanted to be there to love her, guide her and hold her hand in case she stumbled.

Once they left the table and started outside to the backyard, Peggy ran on ahead to the swing dangling from the huge sycamore.

Kerry strolled alongside Jared, who had looped his arm through hers.

"You're probably regretting that you invited Peggy tonight," Kerry commented. "She chattered the whole meal."

"I love Peggy. I never get tired of hearing her talk. She's such an intelligent little thing. I really think she ought to go into law. She already has a command of her words."

Kerry looked at him with surprise. "You say that like you mean it."

He glanced down at her. "I do mean it. Peggy is going to be my daughter. She's going to have my name. Legally. And I want her to have the best education. The best of everything. Just like I want it for you."

She swallowed as a ball of emotions thickened her throat. "Jared, you're going so fast."

"I'm not a guy to sit back on my heels, Kerry. Once I make up my mind I like to go full steam ahead."

"But marriage is serious. And I'd wager a month ago the idea of becoming a husband and father never entered your mind."

He grinned at her. "Of course it didn't," he admitted. "But that was before I saw you."

She groaned. "Oh Jared, I don't know what to think about you."

"All you need to think about is how much you love me."

That wouldn't be hard to do, Kerry thought. Jared was on her mind from morning until night. When she wasn't with him, she felt lost. All she could do was count off the hours until she had the chance to be with him again. She never dreamed she'd allow another man to get this deep a hold on her again. But Jared had a grip on her heart and she didn't see any way of breaking it.

"Jared, come push me, please," Peggy called out.

"I'm coming, honey."

At the swing, Jared gave Peggy several pushes until she was flying high in the air.

"More," she called when he quit.

"No. You don't need to go any higher. You might fall out. Your mother and I are going to sit down on that bench over there and watch you. So you can show us how you can swing yourself. Okay?"

"Okay. And you'd better watch, 'cause I might go really high."

"I'll be keeping my eye on you," he promised, then whispered next to Kerry's ear as the two of them headed toward the park bench positioned near the trunk of the tree. "I think you raised a little daredevil in the disguise of an angel."

Kerry laughed softly. "You don't know the half of it. Before she got lost in the pipe she was into everything. You couldn't turn your back on her for five minutes. But, as bad as it was, the trauma of not being able to get out of that hole taught her a lesson. She understands that things can hurt her."

The two of them sank onto the bench and Jared

quickly slid his arm around Kerry's shoulders and drew her close to his side.

"You look too beautiful tonight, Kerry. Are you trying to torment me?"

Her heart thudded with pleasure as her eyes lifted to his. "I wanted to look nice for you."

"You do, honey. Way too nice. Especially when I can't make love to you."

"Jared," she scolded softly.

He bent his head toward hers. "You know you want to make love to me, too," he murmured.

She breathed deeply as hot memories of their lovemaking flashed through her mind. "Yes."

"Oh Kerry, we've got to get married. Soon. Next week."

Her eyes flew wide. "Jared, I can't marry you now. Like this. We don't have anything settled!"

"What do we need to settle? We love each other. Isn't that all that matters?"

Perhaps it should be, Kerry thought. If she was brave enough maybe she could simply tell him yes. She would marry him in a minute, tomorrow, whenever he wanted. But she wasn't brave. She'd loved and trusted once before and had her world crumble right before her eyes. She'd watched her mother live the bigger part of her married life alone and miserable while her husband hopped from town to town doing odd jobs.

"Of course it matters. I wouldn't marry any man unless I loved him. But I want security, Jared. I want a settled home life."

"And I'll give you that, honey. It just might not be here in Black Arrow," he said.

Sighing, she turned her eyes on Peggy, who was doing her best to pump the swing higher. For the past four years she'd worked hard to make a home for her daughter, to sink roots and keep their lives on a steady course. It terrified her to think of ripping all of that up for the unknown.

"Jared, you don't know where you'll be going or when."

"No. But what does that hurt?"

She looked at him in disbelief. "In other words when your job calls, you expect me to pack up and leave my job and everything behind to go with you."

He frowned. "You make it sound like I'm selfish and uncaring."

She slipped her hands around his and squeezed his fingers. "No. I don't think you're selfish. I just don't think you're ready to be a husband."

Anger spurted through him and he turned his head away from her and drew in a deep breath. "I'm beginning to think you don't want to be a wife. To me or anyone." He looked at her, his blue eyes filled with pain and frustration. "I think if everything was perfect—if my job, my home would always keep us here—you'd still be afraid to commit to me. You've got it in your head that I'm still a playboy. That in the end, I'll let you down like Damon and your father."

She swallowed as tears burned her throat. "I can't argue with you, Jared. I am afraid. I'm sorry, but I am. Please try to understand."

He heaved out a heavy breath. "And what am I supposed to do while I'm trying to understand? I love you, Kerry. I want you. Can't you understand that?"

She nodded glumly. "Yes. I do. And I— Oh, I think the best thing for me and Peggy to do right now is go home."

He tightened his hold on her hands. "I don't want

you to leave. Running away isn't going to fix anything."

"Staying doesn't seem to be fixing anything either," she pointed out miserably. "And I don't want us to argue and spoil the rest of our evening."

His lips suddenly twisted to a crooked grin. "I don't want us to argue either. So I won't mention marriage for at least another thirty minutes."

How could she stay vexed with him, she thought, when just a little grin was enough to melt her heart. "You're crazy. You're awful," she said softly.

He brought his forehead against hers. "Yeah. But you love me anyway."

"Yeah. I guess I do."

He moved closer and touched his lips to hers. "I'll settle for that much right now," he said, then easing back, he stroked his fingers down the side of her face. "And anyway, I have something else to talk to you about."

Her brows arched upward. "Really? I thought you had a one-track mind."

He chuckled, but she noticed the amused look on his face didn't last for long.

"Bram came by this evening. Shortly before you and Peggy arrived. He had news about the fire investigation."

She looked at him with dread. "Oh. Is the inspector wanting to question us?"

Jared shook his head. "No. Thankfully, Bram handled that part of things. From what he says the inspector realizes we were totally innocent bystanders."

Kerry breathed a sigh of relief. "That's wonderful. Then the whole thing was just an accident that happened to occur while we were there?"

His features tight, Jared shook his head again. "Nothing about it was an accident, Kerry. Someone sloshed the place with gasoline, then tossed on lighted candles."

She stared at him with shock. "Oh no, Jared. That's—it's too evil to even think about. I can't believe someone would do that—not while we were in there!"

"But they did, Kerry. I told Bram there was no way the person couldn't have known we were in the next room. The light was on. We'd been talking. You even walked down the hall to the rest room and back."

She shivered as her mind retraced that last night they'd been in the courthouse. "That scares me, Jared. Whoever it was—he could have grabbed me. You might have never known where I was. Or smelled the fire before it was too late!"

"Don't think about that part of it now, Kerry. But I do want you to be extra careful. Like tonight. I'm going to follow you back home. Just to make sure someone isn't on your tail."

Her brown eyes grew dark with fear before they darted out to where Peggy had left the swing to pick clover blooms from the thick blanket of grass beneath the tree. "But Jared, why would someone want to harm me?"

"We don't know that you are a target. But it's obvious the Coltons are. And since you're connected to me you could be caught up in this thing."

She did her best to swallow down the lump of fear in her throat. "What does Bram think about all this? Does he have any leads on who might have set the fire?"

A grimace flattened his lips to a thin line. "Not yet. But I can assure you that he and his department will be working to catch this maniac. Until then, I want you to be very careful. Especially if you go out alone.''

"I will," she promised. "But what about you, Jared. I don't want anything to happen to you!"

The corners of his lips lifted in a brief smile. "I think you actually mean that."

Her fingers reached up to touch his cheek. "I might be afraid to marry you, Jared, but that doesn't stop me from loving you."

He caught her hand and was pressing a kiss in the center of her palm when Peggy came skipping up to them. She had a fistful of clover blooms, but rather than offer them to her mother as she usually did, she thrust them at Jared.

"Thank you, little dove," he told her as he carefully accepted the short white blossoms. "These are the first flowers I've ever had given to me."

Peggy swelled with pride then twirled on her toes before she wedged her way between Jared's knees. "Do you have any ice cream I can eat?"

Jared threw back his head and laughed while Kerry scolded, "Peggy! You're Jared's company. You're not supposed to be asking him for things to eat."

"She can ask me for anything she wants," Jared said, then rising from the bench, he picked up Peggy and set her on his shoulders. "Come on, Mama," he said to Kerry, "I think I have a half gallon of strawberry ice cream just waiting for my little girl to eat."

His little girl. The simple words darted right through to Kerry's heart and as she walked next to Jared and listened to Peggy's shrieks of pleasure, she felt as if her life was snowballing out of control. Peggy had picked the father she wanted and Jared appeared to be champing at the bit to make the three of them a family.

So why wasn't she thrilled about it all? she asked herself. What was it going to take to give her the courage to become Jared's wife?

She didn't know the answer. But there was one thing she was certain about. Jared was not a patient man. He wouldn't wait around on her forever.

Chapter Twelve

"Are you getting ill, Kerry? You've been playing with that French fry for the past ten minutes."

Kerry glanced across the small table at her friend, Christa. The two women had decided to go out to a fast-food restaurant for lunch today, rather than eat a sandwich in the bank's employee lounge.

Kerry shrugged. "No. I'm not ill. I just have a lot on my mind, Christa."

"Peggy's okay, isn't she?"

A rueful smile twisted Kerry's lips. "Oh my daughter couldn't be better. She has Jared wrapped around her little finger. Or maybe he has her wrapped around his. Either way, it's a total love affair."

Christa smiled. "I think that's great. Don't you?"

Another shrug lifted Kerry's shoulders as her expression turned pensive. "You know, after Damon dumped me, I've prayed that a man would come along to love my daughter, to be a good father to her. And I want to think Jared is that man. But I'm—just not sure.''

Christa's brows arched with surprise. ''I don't understand. You just told me they were crazy about each other. It sounds like Jared is very good with Peggy.''

Kerry made a helpless gesture with her hand. ''He's great with Peggy. I can't imagine a man being any better with her. But—''

''All right, what's the matter here?'' Christa prodded. ''You've been acting like you've lost your best friend for the past couple of days. Has something happened with you and Jared?''

Kerry tossed the French fry and wiped her hands on a napkin. ''Jared wants to get married. Soon.''

Christa let out a gasp of surprise, then a bright smile lit her face. ''Boy, he's a quick worker. But I think it's wonderful! Don't you?''

Shaking her head, Kerry thrust a hand through her black hair and pushed the heavy swath away from her cheek. ''I don't know what to think, Christa. I love Jared. But I'm—just not sure he's ready for marriage.''

Christa frowned. ''But why? The man is in his thirties. He ought to know by now if he wants to be a husband.''

''He's thirty-four. And he says his playboy days are over. I believe him when he says that. But I'm not sure he's ready to settle down in the sense of building a home.''

''He has a place here in Black Arrow. Wouldn't you live there?''

Kerry grimaced. ''Not permanently. As soon as Jared's job is finished he'll be moving on to another. And there's no telling where that might be.''

"Oh. So how much longer will he be here in Black Arrow?" Christa asked.

"I'm not sure. I think his job here is winding down. So we might not have much time left to be together."

Christa looked shocked. "But Kerry! Surely you're not going to let Jared's job stand in the way of your marriage? That's crazy! Do you know how many women would kill to be in your position?"

Pain filled Kerry's features. "Look, Christa, I have nothing against Jared's job. He's very good at what he does and he gets top money for doing it. But I have a daughter to think about. I don't want to drag her all over the country from one town, one state to the next. I want a home for us. One that I know will always be there."

Christa reached across the small table and touched Kerry's hand. "But Kerry, home isn't necessarily a place or a house. It's the three of you being together. Haven't you ever thought about it like that?"

"Believe me, I've tried, Christa," she said miserably. "And maybe in the end, I just keep remembering all those promises Damon made that never came through. And my own father rarely ever showing his face in his own home."

"Jared isn't like either one of those men. You shouldn't be comparing."

Kerry shot her a tired look. "Don't tell me you haven't forgotten all the misery your ex put you through. And believe me, Christa, when another man comes into your life you'll see that you can't readily toss all those painful lessons aside. No matter if he is Mr. Wonderful."

Christa made a disapproving click of her tongue.

"You sound bitter, Kerry. Just like your mother. And you always swore you'd never be that way."

For a moment Christa's words brought her up short. Had she turned as bitter and mistrusting as her mother? Dear Lord, she hoped not. Otherwise, she was going to have a miserable life ahead of her.

Glancing at her wristwatch, she said, "It's getting late. We'd better get back to the bank."

Christa looked as though she wanted to say something else but at the last moment decided against it. "Okay, just give me a minute to put on some lipstick. That way my boss might not notice if we're five minutes late," she added with a giggle.

A few moments later, the two women were traveling down a busy street not far from the bank when they spotted a commotion on the next block ahead of them.

"What in the world is going on up there?" Christa mouthed the question before Kerry had the chance. "Looks like a bunch of police cars are gathered at the newspaper office."

Kerry leaned up in the seat. "Slow down," she said to Christa, who was driving. "Maybe we can see what's going on."

As their car crept through the congested area of traffic, Christa said, "Look, there's yellow crime tape all around the front door."

Kerry peered carefully at the group of lawmen standing on the sidewalk in front of the building's entrance. "There's Bram. If the sheriff has been called in on this, it must be something serious."

"Must be," Christa agreed. "Maybe we'll find out something when we get back to the bank." She shook her blond head with dismay. "First the courthouse is set on fire and now the newspaper office has trouble. What in the world is happening to our town?''

''I don't know,'' Kerry replied, but inwardly she was praying this new incident had no connection to the last one. It was already spooky enough thinking someone might be looking over her or Jared's shoulder.

Lunchtime had come and gone when Jared spotted Bram pulling onto the work site. His brother's unexpected appearance surprised Jared. Especially when he knew how Bram had been swamped with work these past few days.

''Looks like you're about to wind things up here,'' Bram said as he joined Jared in an out-of-the-way spot.

Jared gazed proudly out at the ground that had once been strewn and gouged with broken pipes. Now the earth was smooth again and the only thing left was the massive valve which controlled the flow of the gas well.

''Two or three more days,'' Jared told him. ''We've been blessed with dry weather. So that's speeded things up quite a bit.''

Bram sighed. ''I'm glad one of us has had a good break.''

Jared glanced at him sharply. ''Don't tell me something else has happened.''

''The newspaper office was broken into some time during the night.''

Jared's forehead wrinkled with confusion. ''The newspaper office?'' he repeated. ''I wouldn't think they'd have much cash lying around.''

''The perpetrator wasn't looking for money,'' Bram said grimly. ''There was some cash in a small safe in the business office, but it wasn't disturbed. No, it seems this thief was only interested in old papers and micro-film. Any old news that had articles about the Col-tons.''

Jared's jaw dropped as he stared at his brother. ''Oh hell, no. How can you be sure of that?''

''Because the things were strewn around. The piece on when our parents were killed—when you and I and our siblings were born. When Uncle Thomas and Aunt Alice were married and our cousins were born. Do I need to say more?''

Jared's mind was whirling. ''That's the same stuff—''

''The maniac destroyed in the courthouse.''

Shaking his head with dismay, Jared pulled off his hard hat and sank down on the edge of a front bumper on a nearby work truck. ''Bram, this is getting down-right eerie. Not to mention crazy. Have you talked to the rest of the family about this?''

Bram drew in a long breath, then let it out slowly. ''No. But I'm going to have to make some sort of decision. Especially if you say George is already spout-ing off.''

''Well, Aunt Alice and Uncle Thomas have a right to know. And our cousins. George isn't going to say anything to Gloria, he's already made that clear. But Willow knows a little about what's going on. We can't keep it hidden from the rest for very long.''

Bram let out another weary breath. ''You're right. But I would like to have something more concrete to tell them than what we have right now. Which is very damn little.'' He glanced at Jared. ''Look, I have an-other investigation going on right now and I have to go up to Kiowa County to extradite a prisoner this af-ternoon. I was wondering if you and Kerry might be willing to drive out to George's place this evening and go through his old papers, photographs or anything that might shed some light on this mess.''

The only thing Jared wanted or needed to do tonight was be with Kerry. And make love to her until she understood she was going to be his woman. Now and always.

''Sure. We can do that,'' he said, hoping she'd be willing. ''But what about George? Is he home or still with Gran at the feed store?''

''I went by there a few minutes ago. Seems Gran still doesn't feel good, so George doesn't want to leave. I took him aside and talked to him about the papers and things. He doesn't care what you look at. He said anything that had any value at all was stored in boxes in his bedroom closet.''

''Good. I'll go through everything. Although I doubt I'll know what I'm looking for, even if I see it,'' Jared told him, then asked, ''What did George have to say about all this to you?''

''Hell,'' Bram cursed. ''I thought you said the old man knew something. I couldn't get anything out of him that made sense. When I mentioned you and Kerry, he started uttering this stuff about me. That I shouldn't hide behind my Comanche heritage and that one day when I least expect it, I'll hear the coyote's cry and my life will be changed forever.''

Chuckling, Jared lifted both palms in helpless defense. ''Sorry brother, I didn't promise he'd make sense all the time.''

''Just part of the time would be a help,'' Bram said wryly, then gestured toward his waiting truck. ''I've got to be going.''

Jared slapped his hard hat back on and walked

alongside Bram as headed toward his vehicle. "Bram, what does your gut tell you about this—and this stranger looking into our family?"

"As for the stranger," Bram answered grimly, "no one has seen him except Hazel Watkins at the courthouse. And she can't remember much. Brown hair and eyes. Medium build. Nothing noticeable like scars or tattoos. She described him as skulking, but I'm not sure if she means suspicious or rude. In any case, my gut tells me this isn't fun and games."

Jared glanced over at him. "This is one time I wish I didn't agree with you, brother."

When Kerry arrived home that evening from work, the telephone was ringing and no one seemed to be answering.

Tossing down her handbag at the kitchen table, she snatched the receiver from the wall phone.

"Hello. WindWalker residence," she answered breathlessly.

"Kerry, it's me."

Her heart jerked into overdrive. Even though Jared had consumed her thoughts today, she'd not expected him to be calling so early this evening.

"Jared, I'm surprised to hear your voice."

A sensual chuckle came back at her. "I don't know why. You ought to know by now that I'm not going to let much time pass without seeing or talking to you."

Without her even knowing it, a wide smile spread across her face. "I'm not sure I know that, but I'll take your word for it. Why are you calling?"

"I was wondering if you could drive out with me to Granddad's this evening?"

The idea of spending that much time with Jared, especially out in the quiet countryside was enormously appealing, but she couldn't have Peggy out late two nights in a row. Since he already knew her rules about that, he must be expecting her to go on this trip alone with him, she thought quickly.

"I realize you don't want to keep Peggy out late," he went on as though reading her mind. "But actually I—was hoping we could be alone."

A soft rush of breath caught in her throat as heat suffused her body like a warm ocean wave. "Jared—I can't—"

"Don't say can't," he interrupted.

She laughed in spite of herself. "You just used a double negative."

"I have to use double negatives to cancel your single negatives," he reasoned. "And before your mind gets to reading too many naughty thoughts into this invitation, let me tell you I have another reason for you to go. Besides making love to you," he added seductively.

The easy way he talked to her about making love was something new for Kerry. But then everything about having a man like Jared in her life was all new and totally overwhelming. Especially for a Comanche girl who'd lived a somewhat sheltered life.

"Oh," she said guardedly. "What is it?"

"Have you heard about the newspaper office being broken into?"

A sinking feeling hit the pit of her stomach. "Christa and I passed it today on our lunch hour. We saw lots of police around the place, but we weren't able to find out what happened."

"Good. Maybe the general public won't hear the

whole account. They'll just hear that it was a case of simple vandalism.''

Kerry gripped the phone and turned to face the door which led out to the backyard. Through the window, she could see Peggy and Enola in the vegetable garden picking tomatoes. This morning at the breakfast table, her daughter had still been chattering away about Jared and their visit to his house. Kerry had half expected her mother to try to shush the child, but instead Enola had remained painfully silent.

''What do you mean? Was this—something to do with your family?'' Kerry asked.

Jared sighed. ''The perpetrator was looking for certain things,'' he answered bleakly. ''The same things he was after in the courthouse.''

Kerry felt as if someone plunged a fist into her midsection. ''Jared, I've been trying to tell myself that no one was really out to harm us. That the fire was just a coincidence, but now—after this I guess I'd be deluding myself, wouldn't I?''

''I'm sorry, honey, but you would. I understand it's hard for someone like you, who wouldn't hurt a fly, to think of anyone being so malicious, but we've got to face facts. That's why I need your help tonight.''

''Help?''

''Yeah. Bram has asked us to go through Granddad's old papers and photos. He's hoping we'll find some sort of lead.''

''What about George?'' Kerry wanted to know. ''What will he think about us looking at his private papers?''

''He's already told Bram for us to have at it. Besides,'' he added with husky pleasure, ''George isn't going to be there.''

* * *

She should have told him a big fat no, Kerry thought, as moments later she dug through the closet for something to wear. The minute she'd heard George White-Bear wasn't going to be home, she should have put on the brakes. Spending the evening alone with Jared would do nothing to help her clear her mind of the man. And she had to clear it, she told herself firmly. Because she could see a heartache coming.

He said he loved her. But did he really? she asked herself as she stepped into a gauzy white skirt printed with green leaves. He was a man who'd had many women down through the years. It might be that all he really wanted was her body and once he got his fill of that he'd be finished with her. Just as Damon had been finished with her.

Kerry stared at herself in the mirror as she tied the drawstring at her waist. She wasn't a glamour queen by any means. She was a simple Indian girl. She'd always considered her looks forgettable. She couldn't see why Jared would be so taken with her. Especially for a lifetime.

But he says he loves you. He says he wants to marry you.

Groaning at the little voice in her head, she walked over to a chest of drawers and picked up the tiny framed photo of her mother and father when they were young. It was the only photo she had of the two of them and if Enola had her way it would be thrust out of sight.

Wistfully, she touched a finger to her father's grainy image. She'd loved him and wanted his attention so badly, but she'd never really gotten it. After a while he'd become disinterested in his family and drifted away.

If she married Jared, would he do the same thing? she wondered.

Don't think about it now, Kerry. Just think about tonight. Because tomorrow would come soon enough.

"Kerry, I didn't think you could look any more beautiful than you did last night. But you do."

The two of them were sitting side by side on the bedroom floor. In front of them were piles of old photos, letters and an odd jumble of yellowed receipts. For the past two hours she and Jared had pored over every snapshot and every word, each sales slip and other correspondence George had made in the past. Which were precious few considering some of the papers dated back seventy or eighty years.

Still, they'd not seen anything to make them pause and wonder. And they'd especially not seen anything that would make someone set fire to the courthouse or ransack the newspaper office.

"Jared, your attention is wandering," she warned as he leaned even closer and trailed a finger down her bare arm.

"It's been wandering for the past two hours," he whispered. "Wearing that green, you look like a blossom in a field of grass. Do you think I want to look at these dusty old papers, or you?"

Her lips tilted to an impish smile. "I'm not sure."

"Then I'd better make you sure," he said before he dipped his head and covered her lips with his.

In order to keep from toppling over, Kerry was forced to sling her arm around his neck and hang on. When he finally tore his mouth away, his eyes were sparked with fire and his breathing was heavy.

''Do you have any idea how good you taste to me?''
he asked.

The desire on his face and in his voice set her heart
to a fast drumbeat against her breasts. ''You're a
wicked charmer, Jared Colton.''

With one hand supporting her back, the fingers of
the other traced a gentle, seductive path over her forehead, cheeks, nose, then back to her lips.

''No, I'm a man in love,'' he disagreed. ''And I am
in love with you, Kerry. Madly. Completely.''

Being in his arms, feeling the warmth of his skin
and seeing his eyes smiling down at hers made it impossible for her not to believe him.

''Jared,'' she breathed his name, ''I love you, too.
But—''

He interrupted, ''There are no buts, Kerry. I'm not
going to let anything come between us. Not anything.
Understand?''

She didn't. But she wasn't up to arguing with him
tonight. It felt too good to just feel, to simply be Jared's
woman.

For an answer, she lifted her mouth to his. He
clutched her close and kissed her for several moments
until the need to have more of her drove his tongue
between her teeth and a moan deep in his throat sig-
naled the desire boiling up inside him.

The room began to spin around Kerry's head and
her hands clung in helpless surrender to his shoulders.
By the time he lifted his mouth from hers and spoke,
she was trembling from head to foot.

''I think—we need to forget—about these papers,''
Jared said between snatches of breath.

Not waiting for her response, he pulled her to her
feet along with himself, then guided her backwards un-

til they were standing beside an old bed with a scrolled iron head and footboard. A white knobby chenille bedspread covered the mattress.

As his hands worked at the buttons on her green blouse, Kerry glanced over her shoulder at the ancient bed. "Jared, is this your great-grandfather's bed?"

"Yes."

"Uh—" she looked back at him as he began to untie the drawstring at her waist "—we can't make love here."

The chuckle that slipped past his lips was as sensual as the hand cupping her breast. "Why not?"

She couldn't stop the blush seeping into her cheeks. "Because—if we use the bed—he'll know."

He smiled gently down at her as he pushed the thin blouse off her shoulders. "Yes, he'll know. And he'll be very happy."

Happy. It was a word she couldn't help feeling as he switched off the lamp then lay her gently back on the bed.

Much, much later, Kerry was cuddled in the crook of Jared's arm, her head resting on his bronze chest as he stroked her damp hair and smiled into the darkness.

"You know," he said with lazy contentment, "I've been wasting years of my life."

She tilted her head in a way so that she could study his face. "Wasting your life? You seem like you've had a pretty successful one to me."

"Well yes, if you're talking about my career. But I'm talking about all the other things that go on inside a man."

Curious now, she raised up and rested her head on

a bent elbow. "I thought women were the ones who got philosophical after they made love."

He grinned wryly. "I think you just made my point when you said made love. I didn't know what this was all about. In fact, I thought I was the one with the good life. Unattached sex and free to do as I please. But all I was doing was nibbling at the icing. I didn't know how good it was to actually eat the cake, too."

Smiling, she slid her hand across his chest. "Oh. So now I'm just a piece of cake."

For punishment he twisted her onto her back, then with his face hovered over hers, he said, "You're the whole cake, my beauty. You're all the things I never realized I wanted or needed, until I came back to Black Arrow this time and saw your face."

Her heart thudded with both love and dread as she voiced her next question. "But you're going to be leaving Black Arrow. You haven't changed your mind about that, have you?"

A rueful expression filled his face. "No. But we don't need Black Arrow to be happy, Kerry. We just need each other."

She wanted to tell him that it wasn't Black Arrow they needed, but just a spot of their own, a place to call home, not just for today or a month from now, but for always.

"How—much longer do you have on this job?"

"It'll be wrapped up in a day or two. But that's nothing to worry your pretty little head about."

"Jared, you don't understand. I—"

"Kerry," he interrupted, "this time tonight is too precious for us to waste it arguing. Don't you agree?"

It was precious all right, Kerry thought desperately.

Because it might be the last time they were together. Like this or any other way.

"All right," she conceded. "I won't say another cross word."

Chuckling, he brought his lips down to hers. "And I'm going to make sure of it."

Chapter Thirteen

The next evening Jared was sitting in his truck, waiting in the Liberty National parking lot for Kerry to get off work, when his cell phone rang.

Expecting it to be one of his crew, he was surprised to hear Bram's voice. "Hey brother," he said, "what's going on now?"

"Nothing at the moment, thank God. I was just wondering if you and Kerry found out anything at Granddad's last night."

He'd found out he loved Kerry more than he thought humanly possible, Jared thought. Aloud, he said, "We went through stacks of papers and photos, but we didn't see anything that looked odd or suspicious or that might have involved some strange person we didn't know. It was all just simple receipts where he'd bought things at stores here in Black Arrow. Some old photos of our parents and the rest of the family."

"What about Gran? Did you find any of her taken with anyone you didn't know?"

"No. In fact, there were very few photos of her. Which Kerry considered odd since she's George's only child. But I told her that I expect Gran has most of them in her apartment over the feed store."

"That's probably true," he said, then sighed. "I wish we could see them, but I hate like hell to ask her."

Jared paused thoughtfully, then asked, "So you still haven't said anything to her about all of this?"

"No. And I doubt I will. Willow finally managed to persuade her to go to the doctor. Her blood pressure was sky high and he doesn't want her under any sort of added stress. We can't worry her with some maniac digging into the private lives of our family."

"You're right. Making Gran ill wouldn't be worth any sort of clues she might give us. We'll have to get them some other way," Jared said as he quickly reached for the door handle. "Uh—I gotta go, Bram. I'm here in the bank parking lot and Kerry's just come out of the building. I'll talk to you about this later."

He clicked off the phone and quickly slid out of the truck. As he trotted across the parking lot toward Kerry, she spotted him and waved. Even though Jared's heart was thumping with dread, he gave her his best grin.

"What are you doing here?" she asked with an eager smile. Although he was dressed in work clothes and boots, she could see he was clean. Apparently the pipes and trenches no longer required his hands-on scrutiny, she thought.

"Taking you out for a cup of coffee," he said while scooping his arm around the back of her waist.

"Coffee! Jared, it's five in the evening. It's nearly suppertime. And Mom and Peggy will be expecting me home in about ten minutes."

"Okay. We'll eat with the coffee," he said. "And you can call your mother on my cell phone and tell her you'll be late."

"I was late last night," she countered with an impish smile. "We can't have a repeat."

"As much as I'd like a repeat, honey, I have something to talk to you about. I won't keep you out long," he promised.

"Talk? About what?" she asked as he guided her toward his truck.

"Not now. Call your mother first."

Kerry did as he asked, then the two of them walked across the street to a little café that was reminiscent of Woody's, where she'd worked and tried to avoid Jared's flirty advances eight years ago.

In a back booth, they both ordered hamburgers and onion rings then sat back to sip fresh coffee while they waited for their food to be prepared.

"When are you going to tell me what this is all about? Did Bram find the arsonist?"

He reached across the table for her hand. "No. This has nothing to do with any of that."

She watched a frown pull his dark brows together and felt her heart sink. Jared was always happy and upbeat. Even the night of the fire he hadn't looked this somber. Something had happened and she wasn't altogether sure she wanted to hear it.

"Then—what does it have to do with? It must be important for you to cart me away from work before I have a chance to drive home."

"That's because I wanted to talk to you in private."

The last time he'd told her that, he'd confessed that he was in love with her. She couldn't imagine anything more shocking than that.

"Okay. Go on," she urged.

He drew in a deep breath and let it out. "First of all, let me say the site is finished. The boys are smoothing out the last excavation as we speak."

"That's good. I'm sure you're proud to have it finished. And thank God no other innocent child will be endangered by that mess again."

He squeezed her hand. "No. Peggy or any other innocent child can't find trouble there anymore."

Her brown eyes continued to scan his face. "If that's your first news, what's the second?"

He took a sip from his coffee then set the cup back on its saucer. "I've gotten a job offer. A good one."

The heavy weight of dread that had been lounging around in her stomach fell all the way to her feet. "Oh."

His brows arched. "That's all you have to say? Oh?"

She shrugged and found she had to look away from him, otherwise, he might see the tears already burning at the back of her eyes. "I don't know what you expect me to say. Except congratulations."

He glanced around the small café at the diners sitting a few feet away, then leaned forward so that his words were only for her ears.

"Aren't you even interested in where and what it is?"

She blinked and continued to stare at her coffee cup. "Maybe I'm afraid to hear what you have to say," she said in a low voice.

"Afraid?" he repeated in disbelief, then with a frustrated sound he reached for her other hand and pressed them both tightly between his. "Kerry, there's nothing to be afraid of. It's just a job."

That brought her eyes up to his face. "Is it close?"

He shook his head. "West Texas."

A rush of breath passed her lips. "Well," she said in a tight voice, "I knew I'd have to tell you goodbye sooner or later. I guess this just means it will be sooner."

His eyes widened. "Goodbye! There isn't going to be any goodbye, Kerry. You're coming with me. You and Peggy."

She might have known where this was headed, but she had to make it clear here and now where she stood. Otherwise, he'd be forever leading her around from place to place.

"How long will this job last?"

Seeing her question as a sign that she was relenting, his face brightened with excitement. "Six to eight months. A major gas company is going to reroute more than a hundred miles of old pipeline and they want me to head up the engineering on the thing."

Her eyes misted over as she tried her best to smile at him. "I'm impressed, Jared. I truly am. And I'm very proud of you. I just wish—"

"I understand that you want a permanent home, Kerry. But that isn't possible now. And as far as I'm concerned, the most important thing is that we have a home. Together."

Kerry wished she could agree. She wished she could shout with joy and tell him she'd follow him anywhere, but something was holding her back, some fear that she couldn't explain or reason, even to herself.

"I've told you before, Jared, I'm not leaving Black Arrow. Not to become a nomad."

"Kerry—"

"What do you expect of me?" she interrupted. "I have a job, too. I've been working hard these past three years, putting in far more time than is expected of me, so that I can eventually step up the ladder. Do you want me to just throw all that away?"

His head shook helplessly back and forth. "Kerry, I can take care of your financial security. You won't even have to work."

"Look, Jared, I went through years of schooling, just like you did. If I go with you to west Texas, I might as well kiss any sort of high-level job goodbye. As far as that goes, who would hire me when I'm only going to be in town for six or eight months? No one, that's who. I'd do well to get a job as a fry cook!"

He frowned at her. "You're being a little bit over-dramatic here, aren't you?"

"No!" she shot back at him. "I'm being realistic. Something you're—incapable of!"

He started to make a reply, but the waitress appeared with their burgers and he was forced to release Kerry's hand and lean back in his seat. But once she'd served them and went on her way, he said, "You might look at it as an opportunity to spend more time with Peggy. And with me," he said gently.

She suddenly felt so awful it was all she could do to keep from bursting into tears. Instead she had a plate of food sitting in front of her with a throat so choked she'd never be able to swallow a bite.

"Now you're making me sound selfish."

He sighed. "I'm not trying to," he said. He reached for the salt and pepper shaker and Kerry watched him go through the motions of adding the spices to his food. Apparently he wasn't going to let a little thing like their breakup interfere with his eating.

In an effort to appear just as unaffected, she reached for an onion ring and forced herself to take a bite. "Well, the way I see it the only choice left for us is to have a long-distance relationship."

"Like hell," Jared retorted. "I'm not going to settle for seeing you only on weekends now and then. That just won't do. It won't do at all."

She made herself bite into her burger. Eating had to be better than crying, she told herself. "Then I guess we won't have any sort of relationship," she said huskily.

He stared at her, his gray eyes wounded and accusing. "Did last night mean nothing to you?" he asked.

His question was like a whack to her midsection. Beneath the table, she pressed a hand to her stomach. In a strained voice, she answered, "That you even ask such a thing is insulting to me, Jared. You know how I feel about you. I—I'm not like the women you've known in the past. And maybe that's why—you don't understand where I'm coming from!"

His nostrils flared as he turned his gaze back to the food on his plate. "Oh, I think I know where you're coming from. Your problem isn't with me or my job. It's with yourself. You're too busy worrying about the past, to take a chance on being happy with me."

Kerry reached for her purse. "Enjoy your meal and your life," she muttered, then rose from the booth and walked quickly out of the café.

The next five days were the most miserable Kerry had spent in her entire life. Each morning she woke thinking about Jared, missing him and grieving for all they had lost. Her work at the bank was suffering, too. It was almost impossible to keep her mind on percentages and interest rates when all she could think about was never seeing Jared again. Of course it didn't help matters to have Clarence asking about her new beau, or Peggy begging her to go see Jared.

So far, Jared had not come by the bank or her house. The fact deflated her even more, but then she didn't know what she expected. He called every evening, and every evening she'd had her mother tell him she was out. Which he very well knew she wasn't. Kerry hadn't gone out until he'd come into her life.

"Kerry, is that you?"

Kerry tossed her handbag onto the couch and walked back toward her mother's voice in the kitchen. "It's me," she called. "I'll be there as soon as I change clothes."

Moments later, she changed from her tailored dress to a pair of jean shorts and pink T-shirt, then went out to the kitchen to help her mother finish preparing the evening meal.

"I was beginning to wonder what had happened," Enola said. "You're a little late from work this evening. Supper's been ready for a half hour."

"I was finishing up some work I'd promised for Clarence," she explained. Seeing that her mother already had the food on the table, she went to the sink and washed her hands. "If everything is ready I'll get the glasses. You go ahead and sit down."

Enola nodded, then stuck her head out the back door and called to Peggy. The realization that they could let Peggy play in the backyard unattended now was a reminder of how much Jared had changed their lives.

Now her daughter couldn't be coaxed away from the house by wild horses.

Moments later, Peggy came crashing through the door to make a beeline toward her mother.

Kerry stopped what she was doing to kneel down and give her daughter a big hug.

"Hi, Mama," Peggy greeted her, smacking a wet kiss on Kerry's cheek.

"Hi yourself, kiddo."

With her arms still circling her mother's neck, Peggy asked hopefully, "Can we go see Jared tonight, Mama?"

Pain lanced through Kerry's chest. "No, honey. I told you, Jared is busy now. He's going to a new job and he has lots of things to do."

"But when are we going to see him?" she persisted. "I want to tell him about Fred. That he's so smart he can roll over and sit up when I tell him to. Jared will want to know that, Mama."

Hopefully her breaking heart wasn't evident on her face as she tried to give her daughter an encouraging smile. "I'm sure he would want to hear about Fred, but right now it's time for us to eat."

Thankfully, Peggy let the subject of Jared drop and the three of them ate the meal of fried catfish, field peas and corn bread with only simple small talk to break the silence.

Afterwards, Kerry washed the dishes for her mother, then quietly retired to her bedroom.

A few miles away Jared stared at the packed boxes piled in the middle of his living room. Normally he was always excited about packing up and heading out for a new job. He'd always liked the adventure of seeing new places and faces. But this time his heart wasn't in it. He was dreading the moment when he would finally have to drive away from Black Arrow and leave Kerry and his heart behind.

With a weary sigh, he glanced at the telephone on the end table to the right of him. He could try one more call, he thought. But what good would it do? She obviously wasn't answering the phone and her mother was filtering his calls.

The idea that she refused to talk to him stabbed him like a knife blade. He could have sworn that she loved him. Each time she'd touched him, kissed him, made love to him, he'd felt her heart giving to him in a way he'd never felt from any woman. Had he misjudged her so completely?

The agony of his thoughts pushed him restlessly to his feet. He walked out to the backyard and sat down on the bench that he and Kerry had shared only a few evenings ago. The yard was quiet without Peggy's shrieks and giggles and the bench was very, very empty without Kerry beside him.

Any place you go will be empty without Kerry and Peggy.

The taunting little voice in his head had him dropping his head in his hands. What was he going to do, he wondered miserably. What could he do to make her see they were meant to be together.

As the question roiled around in his head he was suddenly struck by a memory so vivid he gasped and squeezed his eyes tightly shut.

Suddenly he was eleven years old again and he was out at his great-grandfather's farm. He'd been helping the old man feed the chickens and as they'd scattered the chopped corn over the bare ground, a white dove had flown down to perch on a nearby fence.

Jared had never seen a white dove before and he'd stared at the bird in total fascination. Then to his total amazement, George had walked over to the fence and held up a palm full of grain to the dove.

Instead of flying away, as Jared fully expected, the bird had hopped onto George's outstretched arm and pecked at the morsels of corn until they were all gone, then it had flown into a nearby tree and cooed forlornly.

"The dove is a lonesome bird without its mate," he'd said to Jared. "One day you will learn that, my boy. One day you will find a white dove of your own and she will bring you great happiness."

As the memory lingered in his vision, Jared's head jerked up and he stared at the empty swing where Peggy had giggled so happily. Chenoa—his little dove. He'd found her and she'd led him to the greatest love of his life! Dear God, his great-grandfather had been right—he didn't know how or why, but somehow he'd known all those years ago.

Not waiting another second, Jared jumped to his feet and headed around the house to where his pickup truck was parked. He might have one hell of a fight on his hands, but now he was more than certain he had the Great Spirit on his side. Kerry was meant to be his wife and some way he had to convince her!

More than an hour later, she was trying to focus on a paperback novel when her mother lightly knocked on the door facing.

"Yes," she called from where she sat propped against the headboard and a couple of pillows.

Enola stepped into the room and Kerry watched with

surprise as she shut the door behind her. They never shut doors in this house. One room simply flowed into the next.

"I wanted to talk to you for a few minutes," Enola explained, "and I don't want Peggy to overhear what I have to say."

Kerry sighed. "Mom, I'm not really in the mood for a serious conversation. Has Peggy been giving you problems? If she has—"

"Peggy has been an angel. It's my daughter that's giving me problems."

Kerry immediately scooted to an upright position and looked at her mother. "I haven't done anything—"

"That's right," Enola interrupted again. "You haven't done anything for days now and I'm wondering why."

Kerry's gaze dropped to her crossed legs. After her argument with Jared in the café, she'd told her mother what had happened and that their relationship was over. At the time Enola hadn't made any comment, other than to say she was sorry. So it surprised Kerry that Enola wanted to speak of it now.

"If you're talking about Jared, I don't know what you're expecting me to say. I thought—" She lifted a doubtful look at her mother. "Aren't you happy that I'm not seeing him anymore? After all, you tried to warn me that he was going to break my heart. Aren't you glad you can now say I told you so?"

Enola walked over and sat down on the edge of the bed beside her daughter. "I never thought my daughter would be a quitter."

Kerry's mouth fell open. "A quitter! What are you talking about?"

"I'm talking about you and Jared. I thought you loved the man."

Still amazed by the direction of their conversation, Kerry stared at her. "I did. I do!"

"Then why aren't you doing something about it? Instead of moping around here like there's been a death in the family."

There had been a death, Kerry thought, the death of her future happiness. "Because there's nothing I can do about it," she answered. "Jared's leaving for a new job. He doesn't want to have a long-distance relationship and I don't want to live a nomadic life."

Enola had never been a physically demonstrative person so it surprised Kerry when she reached over and stroked a hand over her hair.

"Kerry, since you've been a small girl, I've never seen you so miserable and unhappy. Even when you went through that nightmare with Damon. That can only mean one thing—that you must love Jared very much."

The pain in Kerry's heart was so great she bent her head and closed her eyes. "I love him so much, Mom. I don't know how I'm going to live without him."

"Why would you have to? Jared wants to marry you, doesn't he?"

"Yes. But what sort of life would we have? Moving from one job to the next. Never knowing where our next house or apartment will be. That's not what I want for Peggy. Or myself."

Enola reached for her daughter's hand. "Kerry, I admit that I said some bad things to you about Jared. And maybe I would still be saying them now if you hadn't said what you did to me."

Kerry was totally blank. "What I said to you?"

Enola nodded. "Yes. When you asked me if I wanted you to be happy, like me. At first I didn't understand how you could have said such a horrible thing to me. But then I stopped and realized that you were right. All these years I've felt angry and cheated. I blamed your father for ruining my life and eventually I began to see something bad in all men. I was wrong."

Never in a million years would Kerry have expected to hear those words from her mother's lips.

"Mom, we both know Marvin wouldn't have won any husband or father awards. You have a right to feel like you do."

Enola shook her head. "No. I should be feeling guilty and I do."

"Guilty!"

"Listen Kerry, I've always blamed your father for our miserable marriage. But after what you said…well, it opened my eyes and I could see my part in it, too. No, your father wouldn't have won any family awards, but I wasn't the perfect wife either. Oh, I thought I was…at the time. Just like you think you're doing the right thing now with Jared. But you're not, Kerry. Just like I wasn't right when I refused to follow your father to a job he wanted right after we were married."

The implication of Enola's words were slowly pulling back a black curtain and she was desperate to see everything about her father's life that had been cloaked behind it.

"What happened?" she asked.

Enola sighed. "I thought it was more important to stay here in Black Arrow, to buy a house, to stay put, to build a home. I couldn't see that we needed more things than that to make us happy. I needed to see that we *both* had dreams."

Kerry's heart was suddenly filled with tears for everything her mother had lost and her father, too. "Oh Mom, you've never said anything about this before."

Sadly shaking her head, Enola said, "That's because I didn't think it was important. I didn't know it was important until I realized you were making the same mistake I made. And I don't want that to happen to you, Kerry. If Jared is the man you love you need to go to him and tell him you're willing to follow his dreams."

"But Mom," Kerry practically wailed, "do you hear what you're saying? You're telling me to follow his dreams. What about mine? Do I have to give them up?"

Enola surprised her by laughing softly. "No, my daughter. I think that you will both have to make compromises along the way to fulfill both of your dreams. Neither of you can have everything be perfect."

It took several long moments for Kerry to understand what her mother was trying to tell her and when she finally did, she flung her arms around Enola's neck and quietly wept.

"Oh Mom, I love you. Thank you for opening my eyes. I only hope Jared will forgive me for being so stubborn, that he hasn't left without me."

"Mama! Mama!"

The sound of her daughter's shrill call had Kerry going over to open the door. Peggy was dancing on her toes, her little face completely serious.

"Mama! Jared is on the porch and he says if you don't come out to see him he's gonna come in and get you!"

Instant joy surged through Kerry, then just as quickly she was cold with fear. Jared might not be here to tell her he still wanted to marry her, he could be here to tell her a final goodbye, she thought sickly.

She glanced hesitantly back at her mother. Enola smiled and motioned for her to go and go quickly.

With Peggy's hand in hers, Kerry walked to the front of the house and pushed through the screen door. Jared was standing at one end of the porch with his back to them, but the moment he heard their footsteps he whirled around to greet her.

Kerry swallowed and moved tentatively toward him. "Hello, Jared," she said. "Peggy said you wanted to see me."

He wanted to do more than see her, Jared thought. He wanted to jerk her into his arms and kiss her until the only words she could breathe were, I love you. But Peggy was glued to her mother's side and after a week of cold silence from Kerry, he was no longer sure how she felt about him.

"I've been trying to tell you that all week," he said grimly. "Why wouldn't you take my calls?"

She looked hesitantly down at Peggy, then back to him. "Why don't we go around to the back of the house? There's a porch swing there that we can sit in and have some privacy," she suggested to him, then to Peggy she said, "Honey, I want you to go in and tell your grandmother where Jared and I will be."

"Okay, Mama!"

Kerry watched her scoot into the house before she turned her attention back to him. Jared was instantly struck at how beautiful she was to him. Even in a pair of shorts and a T-shirt there was a regal grace about her that came from deep within.

"Let's go on back before I explain anything," she said to him.

Trying to hide his impatience, he nodded and motioned for her to lead the way. A small porch, much like the front, was fastened to the entire back of the house. On one end was a porch swing made of varnished cedar and padded with flower-covered cushions.

Once they were seated, he looked at her and waited until she'd drawn in a deep breath and let it out before he spoke.

"Kerry, I—"

"Before you—"

Their tangled words made them both pause before Kerry was the first to try again.

"Jared, I—why are you here?"

His brows inched upward as though he couldn't believe she was asking such a question. "Why do you think?"

Her troubled eyes searched his face. "To say goodbye?"

Jared couldn't stand it any longer, he had to feel her hand in his, the warmth of her fingers curling trustingly around his. When he reached for her, he felt a sense of relief when she didn't try to pull away.

"Is that what you want, Kerry?"

She was suddenly so overcome with guilt, she couldn't say anything. She'd put him through hell. And in doing so she'd made her own self miserable. Bending her head, she blinked at the tears burning her eyes.

"I feel so awful, Jared. You can't know how awful."

He let out a heavy breath. "This past week has been a nightmare for me, Kerry. I didn't know a human being could be so heartbroken and still be alive. I've been such a bear that my family and work crew wants to disown me. I can't let us part this way, Kerry. I don't care what you say, I—''

Her head jerked up. ''Jared, please. Just stop. Let me talk,'' she pleaded.

''Kerry, I don't want to hear any more of your arguments. If I have to compromise this job—if your job is more important, then—''

''No!'' she blasted out. ''Just hush and let me speak, okay?''

Stunned by her outburst, he stared at her and nodded.

Kerry nervously moistened her lips and tried again. ''First of all, I want you to know I was about to drive over to your house to see you.''

He continued to stare at her as if he couldn't quite believe he was hearing her right. ''You were? Why?''

''To apologize to you. To ask you to forgive me.''

He let out a huge groan and then she suddenly found herself crushed against his chest. While his lips pressed kisses all over her face, he whispered, ''Oh Kerry! Kerry! I love you so much, darling. Surely you know I could never tell you goodbye.''

By now tears were streaming down her cheeks. Jared kissed them away while he waited for her to explain this sudden switch in her attitude.

''I wasn't sure,'' Kerry said tearfully. ''I've been so stubborn and blind. I was afraid you might have already given up and turned your back on me.''

He shook his head. ''If that's the way you feel, why wouldn't you talk to me. I've called every evening this week!''

''I'm sorry,'' she whispered. ''So sorry, Jared. But I was so hurt. And I kept thinking if I gave in to you, I'd be giving up everything I ever wanted. But now I understand that giving you up would be losing everything I ever wanted.''

He buried his face in her hair and held her tight for long moments before he lifted his head and looked into her soft brown eyes. ''And what made you change your mind?'' he asked. ''You seemed so adamant in the café the other evening. Especially when you spoke of your job. And all this week I've been asking myself if I was being selfish and that maybe I didn't have a right to ask you to go with me anywhere.''

''Oh Jared, forget all I said about my job,'' she pleaded. ''Maybe at the time I thought I meant all that. But I didn't. I can find a job anywhere. I was just holding on to that excuse because I was afraid…afraid to give in to you.''

''I still don't understand what's made you change your mind,'' he said with a perplexed shake of his head.

Kerry smiled because she knew how much her next words were going to shock him. ''My mother. Only a few minutes before you came we had a long talk and she made me see I wasn't looking at things from all sides. She urged me to go to you.''

His low chuckle was full of disbelief. ''I came over here this evening thinking I was going to have one hell of a fight on my hands. Instead, I find you telling me you still love me. You do, don't you?''

''Yes! Oh yes! I've been sick this past week without you, Jared. I didn't know how I was going to keep on living once you were gone.''

His head shook back and forth in wonder. ''You said your mother changed your mind. How? I thought she thoroughly disliked me.''

She reached up to frame his face with her hands. ''It

wasn't you personally. Mom had been so hurt for so long that she looked at every man in a bad light. But...something about you...about us falling in love has opened her eyes, too. You know what she said to me, Jared? She said she couldn't let me make the same mistake that she made with my father. And for the first time in my life I understand that he wasn't always the pitiful man he was when he died.''

He took her hands from his face and kissed both her palms. ''Kerry, I promise with all my heart that I'll never roam or wander away from you for a job or any other reason. And when Peggy reaches school age, I promise we'll come back here to Black Arrow and make a permanent home.''

She looked at him, her heart shining in her eyes. ''Do you really mean that?''

Grinning, he nodded. ''Every word. And in the meantime, I want us to have more children to go with Peggy. I want us to be a real family.'' He smiled delightedly. ''A month ago those words would have never passed my mouth. But you've changed me, Kerry.''

Her soft laughter filled his heart with joy. He wanted to make this woman happy, keep her happy for the rest of her life.

''Jared Colton, once playboy of Black Arrow wants to be a family man. I can't believe I'm hearing you say it.''

Still smiling, he stroked her hair and then her cheek. ''Falling in love with you has made me see things differently, too, Kerry. And this nutcase lurking in the shadows and threatening the Coltons has made me realize how special my family is to me.''

''Me, too,'' she agreed. ''The night of the fire...just

the thought of you being hurt or killed made me see I was falling in love with you.''

He groaned with pure happiness, then brought his lips next to hers in a kiss that promised passion and a lifetime of love.

After they'd both caught their breath, Jared let out a husky laugh. ''Maybe I'd better tell you where we're going to be headed next week.''

''Next week? We're getting married and leaving that soon?''

The smile on her face told him tomorrow wouldn't be soon enough and thrill in his heart swelled his chest.

''That's right. And we're going to the Texas hill country, Kerry. Down near Kerrville. It's so beautiful there, honey. It's just like heaven.''

With all her love, she pressed her cheek against his and whispered, ''As long as I'm with you, my darling, any place is heaven.''

Suddenly he jumped to his feet and pulled her from the swing. ''Come on, let's go tell Enola and our daughter the good news.''

Nodding, Kerry clasped his hand and Jared took his first step into the WindWalker home.

*   *   *   *   *

Come back next month to hear

THE COYOTE'S CRY

by Jackie Merritt
(SE 1484, 08/02)

SPECIAL EDITION™

&

SILHOUETTE Romance®

present a new series about the proud,
passion-driven dynasty

THE
COLTONS

**You loved the California Coltons, now discover
the Coltons of Black Arrow, Oklahoma.
Comanche blood courses through their veins,
but a brand-new birthright awaits them....**

WHITE DOVE'S PROMISE by Stella Bagwell (7/02, SE#1478)

THE COYOTE'S CRY by Jackie Merritt (8/02, SE#1484)

WILLOW IN BLOOM by Victoria Pade (9/02, SE#1490)

THE RAVEN'S ASSIGNMENT by Kasey Michaels (9/02, SR#1613)

A COLTON FAMILY CHRISTMAS by Judy Christenberry,
Linda Turner and Carolyn Zane (10/02, Silhouette Single Title)

SKY FULL OF PROMISE by Teresa Southwick (11/02, SR#1624)

THE WOLF'S SURRENDER by Sandra Steffen (12/02, SR#1630)

*Look for these titles
wherever Silhouette books are sold!*

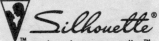

Where love comes alive™

MONTANA MAVERICKS

One of Silhouette Special Edition's most popular
series returns with three sensational stories filled
with love, small-town gossip, reunited lovers, a little
murder, hot nights and the best in romance:

HER MONTANA MAN
by Laurie Paige
(ISBN#: 0-373-24483-5)
Available August 2002

BIG SKY COWBOY
by Jennifer Mikels
(ISBN#: 0-373-24491-6)
Available September 2002

MONTANA LAWMAN
by Allison Leigh
(ISBN#: 0-373-24497-5)
Available October 2002

*True love is the only way to beat the heat
in Rumor, Montana....*

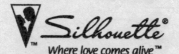

Silhouette®
Where love comes alive™

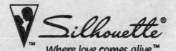

#1483 HER MONTANA MAN—Laurie Paige
Montana Mavericks
It had been eight long years since small-town mayor Pierce Dalton chose work over love. Then pretty forensic specialist Chelsea Kearns came back into his life—and his heart. Pierce hoped that one last fling with Chelsea would burn out their still-simmering flame once and for all. But they hadn't counted on the strength of their passion…or an unexpected pregnancy!

#1484 THE COYOTE'S CRY—Jackie Merritt
The Coltons
Golden girl Jenna Elliott was all wrong for hardworking Native American sheriff Bram Colton, *right?* She was rich, privileged and, most shocking of all, *white*. But Bram couldn't help but feel desire for Jenna, his grandmother's new nurse—and Jenna couldn't help but feel the same way. Would their cultural differences tear them apart or build a long-lasting love?

#1485 HIS EXECUTIVE SWEETHEART—Christine Rimmer
The Sons of Caitlin Bravo
Celia Tuttle's whole world went haywire when she realized she was in love…with her boss! Tycoon Aaron Bravo had his pick of willing, willowy women, so why would he ever fall for his girl-next-door secretary? But then shy Celia—with a little help from Aaron's meddling mom—figured out a way to *really* get her boss's attention….

#1486 THE HEART BENEATH—Lindsay McKenna
Morgan's Mercenaries: Ultimate Rescue
When a gigantic earthquake ripped apart Southern California, marines Callie Evans and Wes James rushed to the rescue. But the two tough-as-nails lieutenants hadn't expected an undeniable attraction to each other. Then the aftershocks began. And this time it was Callie in need of rescue—and Wes was determined to save the woman he'd fallen for!

#1487 PRINCESS DOTTIE—Lucy Gordon
Barmaid Dottie Heben…a *princess?* One day the zany beauty was slinging drinks, the next day she learned she was the heiress to a throne. All Dottie had to do was get a crash course in royal relations. But the one man assigned to give her "princess lessons" was the same man she'd just deposed…former prince Randolph!

#1488 THE BOSS'S BABY BARGAIN—Karen Sandler
Brooding millionaire Lucas Taylor longed for a child—but didn't have a wife. So when his kindhearted assistant, Allie Dickenson, came to him for a loan, the take-charge businessman made her a deal: marriage in exchange for money. Could their makeshift wedding lead to a once-in-a-lifetime love that healed past wounds?

SSECNM0702